The Claus C

CW00864146

FOREVER AFTER

Adam Greenwood

Text and cover design
© Adam Greenwood 2013

First edition published 2013 by

+Saint.Claire+

For my own Mrs Claus
and all those who believe

"Hey Mister!" The words in Nicholai's head sounded familiar, the voice too. It was his own yet not his own. The voice he had had when he was a young boy. "Mister?" the voice came again, a little more worried-sounding this time, "Mister? Are you all right?" Suddenly, Nicholai remembered where he had heard those words before. They were the words he had spoken that day ever so many years ago when, rising early and making his way down to the stables to feed and groom his horse, he had found a strange old man lying in the courtyard of his parents' house.

Satisfied, Nicholai relaxed. He must, he thought to himself, be having a dream, a dream which was incorporating memories for his own past. Although quite why he would be thinking about that incident now he couldn't quite say. He hadn't given that strange but pleasant enough old man a thought in years. The old chap had stayed around for a few days until he got himself sorted out then had been on his way. What was his name? Nicholai couldn't really remember. It had all been so long ago. What he did remember quite clearly, however, were the man's stories. He had actually told some of those in his travels, in the years he had spent walking from village to village and town to town after losing Annalina to the terrible snow.

Someone was shaking him now. Probably Annalina. Nicholai was always a heavy sleeper and his wife often had to shake him awake in the mornings, especially as it never really got any lighter or darker in the network of caves and tunnels they called home so his body received no external prompts as to when it was day or night.

"Mister! Wake up!" the voice was becoming more insistent now, the shaking incorporating itself into the dream. The voice, he knew, would fade as soon as he opened his eyes and, knowing that when he proved hard to rouse, his mischievous spouse was not above splashing him with icy-cold water, he decided to give into her and wake up.

"Oh thank goodness!" the concerned boy said as Nicholai opened his eyes, "I thought you were dead!" The sight that met Nicholai's eyes as he rubbed them and tried to sit up was utterly baffling. There could be no doubt he was in the courtyard of his parents' house, a place he had not visited since he left there at the age of twelve and a place that, he was fairly sure, didn't even exist anymore, not like this anyway. Over the years, in his annual flight, he had seen many changes to the world, none more noticeable than in the place he had once called home.

The grand estate that he was to have inherited had been split amongst various others who, in turn, had passed parts of it to their own children who had either passed it onto others or sold their shares to fund a new life for themselves elsewhere. More houses and other homes had been built in the grounds of his own and the big house itself had passed into the general ownership of the community, becoming first a school, then a library and more recently some sort of centre for business and yet here he was and the place was exactly how he remembered it.

Could he still be dreaming? He looked at the boy who had been so anxious to wake him and all colour drained from his face. He felt hot and cold at the same time and his whole body began to shake. It was...but it couldn't be!

"How..." he managed to stammer, "Who are...am I...how?" he asked feebly before passing out from the shock and collapsing back down onto the cobbles of the courtyard.

Fearing the strange visitor may be badly hurt, the boy ran to the house, only to crash into his father's rather ample belly as the wealthy but kind man opened the door.

"Nicholai?" he asked his clearly-panicked son, "What's wrong?"

One

Nearing the end of his tenth year, there were only two things that Nicholai was completely certain of. The second was that he liked to help people and the first was that he loved Annalina.

A little less than two years his junior, Annalina was the girl that he had loved since the moment he, supported by his mother, had held her as a tiny baby in his arms. The daughter of his mother's cousin, they would be married when they were old enough to join the two families and estates together. Although not as rich as Nicholai's father, Annalina's owned the largest farm for many miles around and was an important, well-liked and respected member of the community. For the young couple, adulthood, and with it the prospect of their marriage could not come fast enough. They spent every moment they could together and were each other's first thought in the morning and last before going to sleep.

The only shadow on their horizon was the prospect that, when he was old enough, Nicholai would have to leave the village and spend two whole years away from her in the city, learning all the skills he would need to manage the vast combined estates to which he would be heir. They both knew that that time of separation would be the most horrible time in either of their lives but that it was sure to pass quickly, after which they could spend the rest of all time together. Neither of them had known, back then, just how long the separation would prove to be or that they would really, once reunited, have the rest of all time to spend together. They were just two young hearts in love both agreed to focus on the time they had together rather than dreading the time when Nicholai must go which, after all, seemed a very long time in the future.

How strange it is that, as we grow older, years seem to flash past in a matter of weeks yet when we are children, to say that something is one year away is to say that is in the far distant future and that something two years hence is really beyond comprehension. So it was that young Annalina and Nicholai, or Nico as she called him, spent the golden days of their childhood in a perpetual present in which they were happy, together and in love.

Together with his father, Nicholai, who was quite tall and strong for his age, lifted the unconscious stranger to his feet and helped him into the house. Although not as bitterly cold as it had been known to get at times, it was still too cold a morning to leave a possibly ill and clearly confused person outside all on their own. In the parlour, near the fire-place, was a large and comfortable sofa. They lay the newcomer down upon it and pulled off his thick, fur-lined boots to make him more comfortable.

Once they had informed Nicholai's mother and the household staff about their new guest and sent to the village for a doctor, Nicholai's father sat down with him and asked his son about how he had found the man and whether he had given any clue as to his identity.

"I've no idea who he is," the young boy explained after recounting how he had practically tripped over the unconscious old man, "I'm not even sure he knows himself. He woke up for a few moments but seemed really scared and confused."

"How about his voice?" asked his father, "Did it sound like he was from around here?"

"A little bit," Nicholai furrowed his brow, "but mixed with all sorts of other accents. He reminded me of the travelling minstrels and the craftsmen who come for the fairs in that way, like they're from one place but have been to lots of others and picked up traces of everywhere they went."

"He's clearly not a poor man," observed his father who went by the name of Claus, son of Nicholai, having named his first and only child after his own father, "Look at his clothes!"

Looking as instructed, Nicholai realised what his father meant. Not only had the boots been made from fine, thick leather and lined with fur but his long red velvet coat was also sumptuously fur-lined and decorated with fine gold embroidery. Beneath the coat he wore a shirt of no special style but clearly made from high quality linen, a vest similar in style to the coat and a pair of brown trousers which looked almost brand new and clearly tailored to a very high standard. Although somewhat eccentric in appearance, the man was clearly anything but poor.

"I wonder what he was doing out there then?" Nicholai pondered, "I didn't see any kind of cart or even a horse. Nothing like that at all. Just him."

"There was a storm last night," Claus reminded him, "Quite a bad one too. The worst I've seen since before you were born but, strangely," he mused, "there doesn't seem to be much sign of it this morning. I expected there to be much more but, from what I saw just now, there's hardly any."

"You think he got lost?" asked Nicholai, looking again at the man laid out, still unconscious, on the couch.

"Must have done. Lost his horse or got separated from the rest of his party. Probably climbed over the gate hoping to seek shelter with us for the night but collapsed before he could reach the house.

"The Doctor's here!" Nicholai's mother, Greta, announced with a smile, showing the small, harassed-looking man into the parlour. "You'd better go see to your horse," she reminded her son, not unkindly, "he'll be missing you. We'll stay with the Doctor while he checks over our new friend and when you come back we'll hopefully be able to tell you a little more."

Pausing to give his mother a big hug, Nicholai did as she suggested while the Doctor knelt beside the couch and opened his bag. First he listened to the man's heart-beat which seemed to be regular enough, checked his head for any signs of trauma but found none and finally pulled open each eye in turn to check for the tell-tale signs of concussion. Although the man did not wake up during the examination, the Doctor saw nothing that gave him cause for concern.

"Well," he said, after the examination was complete, "there doesn't seem to be anything wrong with him. Medically he's as fit as a fiddle. I'd say he's probably had some nasty shock of some kind and just needs to sleep it off. He should be fine in a day or two. Are you able to put him up here for the time being or should I see about finding a hostel of some kind?"

"Oh no, that's no bother." Claus smiled as Greta nodded, "He's more than welcome to stay here while he gets back on his feet. It will be no trouble at all."

"Good," smiled the Doctor, "all he needs is rest and some good food which I know," he grinned at Greta, "that he will definitely get here! There's just one slightly strange thing."

"Oh?" Greta asked, "What's that?"

"Well," the Doctor explained, "When I first saw him, with his white hair and beard, I took him to be an older gentleman, well into his fifties, but looking at his face more closely and judging by his general physical condition, I would say that he is no more than thirty. Thirty two or three at the very most. It seems odd that his hair should have lost its colour so completely at that age but then," he smiled again and closed up his bag, "the human body is a strange and marvellous thing, replete with mysteries all of its own!"

"So," Greta turned to her husband after paying the Doctor and seeing him to the door, "I suppose we need to get a room made up for him and I should start a pot of soup for when he wakes up! He looks familiar somehow, but I couldn't say why."

"I know what you mean," Claus nodded, "There's something about his face that just seems, well, like I've seen it before but I've no idea where. I just wish we knew his name!"

Two

"Guess who!" came the cheeky question, accompanied with the obligatory hands over his eyes. Nicholai, knowing full well who it must be, still went along with the customary game that was expected of him every time his young sweetheart played this trick on him.

"Hmmm," he pondered loudly, dropping the brush with which he had been grooming his fine white horse to the ground, "I wonder who it could be? Is it perhaps the vicar, come to check I've said my prayers?"

"No!" came the giggling reply. "Guess again!"

"Then perhaps the baker?" Nicholai guessed, "Come to bring me a bun for my breakfast?"

"One more guess!" the voice behind him challenged.

"Hmmm, now if I have only one more guess, I must think very carefully!" Nicholai teased, "I would say it was the Doctor if not for the fact that he was here earlier, and I have only just had new shoes so it can't be the cobbler. It's just possible that it is my tutor bringing me extra work but you don't smell as bad as he does!" The person behind him giggled again, enchantingly, "I know!" Nicholai exclaimed as if he had just received a sudden epiphany, "It is the farmer's daughter, come to give me a kiss!"

"Yay!" Annalina grinned, removing her hands from her beloved's face, "I was worried you'd never guess!"

"Well it was a close thing," Nicholai chuckled, turning to see his future wife, "After all, I almost ran out of guesses! I hate to think what would have happened if I'd not guessed it right that last time!"

"Then I'd have just had to go away and not come back until tomorrow." Annalina informed him sternly, her hands on her hips. "And you wouldn't have got your kiss!"

"Well then," grinned Nicholai, "It's a very good job I guessed correctly!"

Unable to wait any longer, Annalina flung her arms around Nicholai's neck and kissed him hard on the lips. When the kiss was over, Nicholai stepped back to get a good look at his sweetheart. Despite having known her all her life, every time he saw her, her beauty took his breath away.

She was a fair bit shorter than him but what she lacked in size she made up for in spirit. Her long, flame red hair was, as usual, worn in a long plait which hung over one shoulder. Her big, green eyes were sparkling with energy and happiness and she was dressed in a light brown wool skirt and a dark red corset over a plain white blouse. Every day she looked more beautiful than the last and this day was no exception.

"What did you mean just now, by the way?" she asked, her head tilted slightly to one side, "When you said the Doctor had just been. Is someone in your family sick? Or one of the servants? It's not Joseph is it?" she asked, her eyes wide with worry. Joseph was the grounds-keeper of the estate and lived in a small cottage a few minutes' walk from the big house. He had children of his own, around the same age as the young couple, and both of them considered him like a second father, someone they could go to when they had any problems or needed to talk about something. They knew they were always welcome in his cottage which was a place of love and happiness and the thought that something might have happened to him made Annalina want to cry.

"Oh no!" Nicholai assured her, brushing a stray lock of fringe out of her face, "Nothing like that. There was a man sleeping out here this morning. We think he got lost in the storm last night. He couldn't tell us who he was or why he was there but we got him inside to keep him safe. We called the Doctor to come and check that he wasn't hurt or anything and the Doctor says that he's fine, just needs to take it easy for a few days. In fact," he grinned, grabbing her rather cold hand in his warm one, "he's probably woken up by now. Let's go and say hello!"

Three

"Mama?" Nicholai asked as he pulled Annalina into the parlour by her hand, "Is he awake yet?" He did not have to wait for an answer as, moments after entering the room he saw that the man was now sitting up, his coat laying over the back of the sofa but a blanket around his shoulders, clutching a bowl of Greta's delicious soup in his hands.

"Ah!" his mother turned and saw them entering the room, hand in hand. "I wondered how long it would be before you came to see what was going on. Nice to see you, sweetheart." Annalina dropped Nicholai's hand and hugged her aunt who greeted her with a kiss on the forehead. The young girl loved that, despite the fact that she visited at least once every day, usually more, and sometimes even spent whole days there, her aunt always seemed pleased to see her as if her arrival was a nice surprise.

"This is my son," Greta informed the man, who looked up from his soup and smiled warmly, "He's the one who found you."

"Well," smiled the man, his voice far more relaxed and less anxious than before, "it would seem I owe you a debt of gratitude. What's your name, my fine fellow?"

"Nicholai." the boy replied, "And this is Annalina, my cousin." He pulled the girl forward and she gave the visitor a polite bob of a courtesy.

"A pleasure to meet you both," smiled the man, nodding his head in acknowledgement, "My name's Ni..." he paused, as if, for a second, he had forgotten his own name, "Nicholas." He smiled. "My name is Nicholas."

"That's almost the same as my name!" Nicholai grinned.

"And a very fine name it is too!" the man confirmed.

"Can I leave you in the care of these two for a few minutes?" Greta asked, "I have to go and make sure everything is ready for you upstairs, for later, and see if I can find you some clothes that might fit." Although she had plenty of servants who would be able to deal with such business for her, there was something about this man that made her want to take care of him personally. It was an almost parental feeling which she knew was silly as he was only a few years younger than herself.

"I'm sure we'll be fine," he assured her, "but please don't go to any trouble on my account. What you have done already is kindness enough." His eyes were wide, a little tearful, but he continued to smile reassuringly and Greta left the room, reminding the children to take care of him and to be polite.

"Now," the man who had introduced himself as Nicholas smiled, "why don't you come and tell me a little about yourselves?" He patted the cushions either side of him, inviting Annalina and Nicholai to come sit. "Nicholai?" he asked, confirming the name, "And Annalina?" they both nodded. "That's a very pretty name." he smiled again, warmly. Annalina grinned as she and her beloved sat down beside the strange but interesting new visitor. Both felt instinctively that he was someone they could trust and someone that they wanted to find out more about. "Correct me if I'm wrong," Nicholas asked, "but I suspect you two are more than just cousins?"

"Oh yes!" Annalina grinned broadly, blushing a little.

"We're to be married as soon as we're old enough! When Nicholai has been to the city to complete his education."

"Ah yes," the man nodded, a far-away look in his eyes, "I remember."

"Remember?" Nicholai titled his head and furrowed his brow, "What do you mean? We've only just met."

"Sorry," smiled the man, "I meant I remember when I was your age. I was in a very similar position myself. Young, full of life and ever so much in love!"

"What happened?" asked Annalina, intrigued, "Did you get married?"

"Oh yes!" the man assured her, "A little later than we had planned. Other things rather got in the way and we were separated for a lot longer than we expected, but eventually we found each other again. Now we are married, ever so happily!"

"Does your wife know where you are?" Nicholai asked, "Won't she be worrying about you?"

"She knew where I was going the night I set out," he answered, sadly, "I don't know how long it will take me to get home to her. She was expecting me to be gone for some time, I suppose, but if I can't get back in time then yes, she probably will start to worry."

"Why would you be gone for so long?" Nicholai asked.

"For my work," the man explained, "I make a trip once a year. It doesn't really take all that much time but it seems to her like I'm gone much longer."

"I understand that." Annalina looked a little sad. "One time, Nicholai had to go into the city to the hospital and he was gone for two days. It seemed like forever!"

"When you have good friends around you," the man smiled but a little sadly, "you learn to cope. During the time we were apart before, my wife made some very good friends and together they went through a lot. I'm sure they will help her now."

"What's her name?" asked Annalina, liking the sound of the lady to which this visitor was married.

"Annabelle." he told her, smiling. Annalina grinned at the similarity to her own name. She was sure that she had never met this man before but, as with Nicholai's parents, she found him very familiar, as if she had known him a long time ago. Perhaps he had relatives in the village, she wondered, people that she might know. Although, try as she might, she could not put her finger on who he reminded her of.

"Are you from around here?" Nicholai asked, apparently having the same thought. "You sound like you might be."

"I was," the man admitted, "a very long time ago. I'm a lot older than you probably realise."

"Has the village changed much since you lived here?" asked the boy, curious to find out more about this visitor and possibly the history of his own home.

"Since I lived here?" Nicholas chuckled, "More than you can imagine yet, when I look around me," he cast his eyes around the room, that same far-away look on his face, "it seems hardly to have changed at all."

"So what will you do?" Annalina took his hand and squeezed it, "How will you get home to her?"

"I'm not sure," he shook his head, "I know I must get home somehow. The trouble is, I really don't even know how I got here. It shouldn't have been possible. If I can find out how I got here then I can find out how to get back."

"Do you have friends you can contact?" Nicholai asked, "People who might be able to help you get back? I'm sure you'd be welcome to stay here as long as you want or need and we'll do whatever we can to help you but, well, if you don't even know how you got here then I've no idea how we'd be able to get you back."

"You know what?" the man grinned broadly, as if Nicholai had just given him a great idea, "I think that maybe I do! You have a horse, I believe? A fine, strong gelding?"

"That's right!" Nicholai was surprised, "How did you know?"

"I think your mother mentioned it earlier," the man explained, looking a little embarrassed as if he had maybe said something that he shouldn't have, "I'm not sure exactly. I know this is a big thing to ask, but would you mind if I were to borrow him for the next few days? It might help me reach my friends and find out what's been going on. What do you say?"

Normally, there was no way that he would have let anyone else ride his precious Sleipnir. The young boy had named his equine companion after the horse in the stories he so enjoyed reading, although the horse in the stories had eight legs his own steed had the conventional four and Nicholai considered Sleipnir, apart from Annalina, to be his closest friend. Yet there was something about this man that made him feel that he could trust him, even with something so incredibly precious to him.

"Yes!" he beamed, "Of course you can! He can be a bit bad tempered with anyone other than me so I'll have to show you how to handle him."

"Of course." the man nodded, "That is very kind of you. Perhaps, after I've had a chance to rest up a little and decide what I'm going to do, you can take me down to the stables and introduce us?"

Four

A few minutes later, once the children were gone, Nicholai sat sobbing with his face in his hands. This was just all too much to take in. Somehow, he had been thrown back in time to his own childhood. For the first time in his life he knew the identity of the strange old man, the memory of whom had been somewhat eclipsed by the memory of what happened in the weeks shortly afterwards. This, he realised with a start, was only a matter of days before Annalina would be lost in the snow and his life would be torn apart. His young self seemed so happy and content, his love for Annalina obvious at the first glance. When he had looked up and seen her it was all he could do not to run to her and hug her, his one rock of consistency in this strange and terrifying situation. But this was not his Annalina. One day, she would be, but right now she did not even know who she was.

Thinking back, Nicholai was amused to realise that his younger self had always considered the visitor, who he now knew to be himself, as an old man when in fact his physical age was only a little over thirty. Younger in fact than Nicholai's father. It was true that he and his wife had now lived for over three centuries but neither had aged a day since their wedding day when they drank the last of the life-giving elixir distilled from the fruit of the long-ago fallen tree. The tree from whose wood his sleigh was carved. He supposed that the whiteness of his hair and beard were enough to make him appear old to a young boy, especially as children have a tendency to consider any adult old without too much appraisal.

Harder even than seeing Annalina and his younger self had been seeing his parents, young and strong again. He knew that the young lovers were soon to be separated but that, one day; they would find each other again. His parents, however, were about to lose their only son and not see him again until very near the ends of their lives when the elves would bring them to the caves so that they could attend his wedding. They had told him that day that they had gone on to have other children, the families of whom had inherited the estate that was to have been his as he became heir to an even greater legacy, but that would not lessen the pain that they were about to encounter. He wished there was some way he could save them from it, to protect them, but he knew that there was not.

Pondering as he wiped his tears, he wondered if it was even possible to change the past, to re-write the story that had already been written. What if, in trying to change things for the better he accidentally made things worse and destroyed his own future? Although his mortal life had been anything but simple and had included ever so much pain and hardship, it had ended well, leaving him with Annalina in what he could only describe as their own private Heaven. A place where they could be together until the end of time, helping and bringing joy to others as they both so loved to do.

Screwing up his eyes, Nicholai desperately tried to remember what had happened, to see how he had got there. When he was flying his sleigh, time would come to a complete stop for anyone who had not been influenced by the elixir, frustrating the efforts of even the most determined child who intended staying awake to catch a glimpse of him. So it was that, for him and Annalina, the year was three or four days longer than for the rest of the world. The first few years, he had been able to complete his deliveries within what seemed to him to be a little over one day, although to those who received his gifts, of course, it all happened in a matter of moments. As the years had gone on and more and more children had come to expect his annual visit at the darkest time of year, it had taken longer and longer to complete. One benefit of not ageing, they had both found in the weeks after the wedding, was that their bodies no longer needed sleep. Certainly their minds still craved the outlet that dreaming offered and they still enjoyed falling asleep together in each other's arms when they wanted to but, if either of them had to go for extended periods of time without it, they would not become ill as a result. So it was, then, that even though Nicholai's annual delivery now took nearly a week in relative time, he was able to keep going, not having to make regular stops which would have extended his time away from home by many more days.

For her part, Annalina tended not to sleep while he was gone either, preferring to stay busy helping the elves with their many different tasks, beginning to prepare the toys for the next year even before he was home from delivering the current batch. Then, when he arrived back to the caves, they would set the reindeer free back into the forest for another year then all sit down together, Nicholai, Annalina and all the elves, for a great feast. After, of course, the couple had pressed their hands into the indentations on the back of the sleigh to end the enchantment and re-start time for the rest of the world. Once the feast was concluded, they would retire to their bedroom and sleep, often for a whole day, before getting back into the day-to-day routine of life amongst the elves.

While time was no longer frozen, progressing as normal along its path, he had been cast back somehow, back to a time in his life when he had been happy but just before the worst time in his life. Perhaps, he wondered, as he was there and knew what was to happen, he could stop it, make it right again? Had the elves not said that he and Annalina were supposed to have arrived together as adults but that her accident had forced a change of plans? What if he were to somehow stop the children going out to play that day? Or what if he went with them to keep Annalina safe through the storm then return her home once the snow had stopped falling?

But even as the thought occurred to him, he knew that it could not be. He had not altered time by being there, he had always remembered the strange old man who had been around for just a few days before that fateful time, the man who had vanished only two days before Annalina was lost but whose disappearance had been eclipsed in his memory and his heart by the loss of his beloved. This was what had always happened. He'd always been there which meant that he could do nothing to change the course of events as they unfolded. He pondered why it was that the elves seemed to believe that the course of time had been re-written by Annalina's accident, their magic book having apparently told them to await the arrival of a grown couple. They said they had seen the book change to show her in danger and had rescued her but there had always been something about the story that didn't quite add up. If they had only known at the last minute like that then how, without the aid of his sleigh, had they been able to reach her so quickly? One strange quirk of the elves' immortality, Nicholai had noticed over the years, was that their memory of the past was subject to change and influence. Their development frozen as it had been when they were only children had left them with a child's tendency to rewrite their own memories of long-ago events in the way that most adults tend not to. He could only assume that this same tendency did not affect him or Annalina because they had not brought their ageing to a stop until they were fully grown.

Like all children, including himself and Annalina during the time that he was now visiting, the elves lived in a perpetual present where the past was little more than a story and, as such, was fluid and subject to change. Added to this was the fact that, as Nicholai had learned shortly after his arrival at the caves, the book had been made for Annalina and would only work properly for her. While the elves could use it to discern general understanding of events in the past, present and future, only Annalina could control it properly, to demand that it show her what she wanted it to show rather than simply what it thought she needed to see. Perhaps all the elves had actually seen before was the pair of them there together as adults, the time when, after many years of travelling, searching for his lost love, Nicholai had arrived at the caves and they had been reunited. Maybe the book only showed them the circumstances of Annalina's arrival when the time came that they would need to do something about it.

If nothing else, this strange adventure would perhaps allow him to find some answers about what had happened at that time, how the elves had managed to rescue Annalina and take her to their caves which were so very far away. But how was he even there in the first place? He couldn't remember. His brain was too clouded by the many different, simultaneous thoughts, to be able to focus. Instead, he decided to lie down for a short while and hopefully sleep enough to rest his troubled brain.

Five

"He seems to like you." Young Nicholai smiled as the older man took the reins and patted the magnificent beast's neck affectionately. "It's strange; he doesn't normally take to new people so quickly."

"Ah well," chuckled the white-bearded man, his eyes sparkling, "I have something of a way with animals. I used to have a horse when I was a boy. Great, strong beast he was, much like your friend here." He patted the horse again.

"Do you have one now?" asked Nicholai, "Is that how you got here?"

"No," the older man explained with a hint of sadness in his voice, "Where I live now is not so good for horses. I never did find out what became of mine. I left home, you see, when I was not much older than you. I knew I wouldn't be able to look after him so I didn't take him with me. I still think about him sometimes, wonder what he did for the rest of his life."

"He might still be alive." Nicholai observed, "I've heard of some horses living quite a long time."

"It's possible," the man chuckled, patting Nicholai's horse again and teasing a knot out of its mane, "I wouldn't have thought it likely but then," he mused, "I've known some people and animals live far longer than anyone would expect." He gave another chuckle which confused Nicholai a little as he could not see what was funny about it. "I must say," the man continued, "I've found myself rethinking what I consider possible quite a lot today!"

"I promise I won't keep him out too long," he assured Nicholai as he lifted the thick leather saddle from the hook on the wall and placed it carefully on the animal's back before fastening and tightening the straps, "I just need to take a look around the area, see if I can find any trace of my companions or my...coach." He paused before this last word as if he had been about to say something different and had changed his mind at the last second but Nicholai did not think anything of it. "I know I'll be able to cover more ground on horseback than on foot and there's less chance of me getting lost again! Thank you," he grinned and gave Nicholai a firm handshake, "I really do appreciate it."

Throughout the exchange, Annalina had been standing by the stable door, watching the pair as her beloved Nicholai went to great lengths explaining the proper way to handle his companion beast. A young girl, her hair tied up under her cap, was busy in the stables refilling the water troughs and bringing in more hay for Sleipnir and the other horses. Annalina didn't recognise her but this was not particularly unusual. Nicholai's parents kept a reasonably large retinue of permanent servants and other staff but would often hire people passing through the area, or children from the village hoping to earn a little money to help their family, for a day or two. Often, if there really was no work to be had, especially when it came to children, the kind landowners would invent tasks for them to do, rather than sending them away empty-handed, and would pay them handsomely afterwards. This girl seemed to know what she was doing so Annalina assumed that she was one of the other children from the village, possibly connected in some way to the mill or the militia barracks nearby, and had been hired for her useful skills in animal husbandry.

While she waited, Annalina had made light conversation with the girl, who had dark hair and olive skin similar to Nicholai's, in contrast to her flame-red hair and pale, freckled face, but the girl seemed quite engrossed in her tasks and Annalina did not wish to distract her. Finally, after what seemed like hours but was in fact only a few short minutes, Nicholai was done.

"Come on!" she grabbed his hand and pulled him towards the gate on the other side of the courtyard, "I'm sure he knows what he's doing! Look how much Sleipnir seems to like him!" Nicholai looked over his shoulder and saw his well-loved horse happily eating something from the stranger's hand, a sugar-lump or similar treat perhaps. Something that he would never normally do with anyone other than Nicholai himself. "Let's go play in the forest," she tugged his hand more firmly, "I found something really exciting in there the other day and I can't wait to show you!"

Six

Once he was sure that his younger self and Annalina were gone, Nicholai pulled the stable doors closed and stood leaning on them, his arms folded, watching the stable-girl go about her business, her cap pulled down low and avoiding any eye-contact.

"Excuse me," he called to her when it became clear that she didn't intend on acknowledging him, "but would you mind telling me exactly what you're doing here and what is going on?"

"I don't know what you mean, Sir. Sorry." she muttered, still refusing to look directly at him, "If you care to take the horse out now, I can clean out his stall while you're gone."

"I'm not going anywhere," Nicholai informed her, his arms folded and his face serious, "until you tell me what's going on here. Why are you here? Did you follow me?" This time she made no reply. Somewhat exasperated, Nicholai reached out as she came near and pulled her cap off her head. Her long black hair tumbled down around her shoulders but not quickly enough to prevent him catching a glimpse of the pointed tips of her ears. "I know exactly who you are!" he informed her, trying to suppress a chuckle as she looked up in shock, "We've known each other for centuries and that is hardly a heavy disguise. Now would you please, in the name of all that's Holy, tell me why I am here and what is going on!"

"Begging your pardon, sir," the elf stammered, "but we've never met. I know who you are, of course! But I have no more idea as to why you're here than you do!"

"So you did not travel with me?" he asked, starting to suspect the answer.

"No, sir." she shook her head, "I arrived a few days before you did, from my home in the North. There are three of us working on this estate at the moment and another two at the farm."

"I see," Nicholai nodded, pulling up a stool and indicating that she should do likewise, "And why are you here?"

"We've always been here," explained the elf, "Five of us at a time, for only a few weeks each. That way, the people here don't get suspicious and we don't have to spend too long away from home. When you've been together as a family as long as we have, it's very hard to be apart."

"I understand that completely." Nicholai nodded, his voice warm and reassuring. He was already feeling guilty for having been annoyed with her moments earlier but she did not seem to be holding it against him. After all, if she understood who he was then she must also understand how strange, frightening and confusing this situation must be for him. Back in his own time, he knew that the elves had forgotten who they truly were or where they came from until Annalina had read the account left for her in the magic book and, along with the story she had received from the Pieten elder, was able to understand and explain to them their origins. After three centuries of being with Annalina for all but a few days every year, he was feeling her absence acutely and could only begin to understand what it must be like for the elves who had been together since before recorded time. Before, in fact, the human race was quite yet human.

Although very similar in appearance to human children, it did not take a particularly close examination to show up the differences, the most prominent of which were their large eyes, almost one and a half times the size of an average person's which made them ideally suited to life in the dimly-lit caves, and their ears which were large and pointed. They were small too, slightly smaller than typical children of their physical age and although he could not be sure, for he had never seen an adult member of their race, Nicholai did not believe that it would ever have been possible for them to grow to anywhere near his own height and stature. Aside from this, their toes were long and dexterous and their joints more flexible than an average human's, although this could simply have been the result of millennia of perfect health and peak physical fitness.

Distantly related to the elves, he knew, were the Pieten – a tribe of small wiry men, covered from head to toe in black hair, almost ape-like in appearance but with an intelligence, creativity and language which marked them out as far closer to man than beast. They were the distance ancestors of modern man and the elves represented a link between the two, a marker of the journey from Pieten to man.

"We have been here from the beginning," the rather timid elf continued her story, "since you were born. We came here to watch over you, and later the little miss too. We saw in our book that the Chosen Ones had become manifest and we needed to make sure that nothing happened to you before you were able to find us."

"I see." Nicholai nodded, stroking his beard as he always did when thinking over a difficult problem. Although very familiar to him in his own time, this elf clearly did not know him personally. Although he considered the elf before him as a close friend, as family, Nicholai understood that he was meeting her at an earlier time in her life, a time before they had officially met. Her plan to remain unnoticed must have worked well as he had no memory of her from this time and wondered, with a start, how many other chance encounters of his childhood had actually been with the elves sent to watch over him.

Since she was clearly a part of the world to which he had travelled rather than the one from which he had come, Nicholai thought it would be unfair of him to tell her about the tragic events which were to unfold within the next week or so but that was no reason that he couldn't enlist her help now. She knew who he was and therefore knew that he had been displaced from his own time so he was sure that she would be willing to help him find his way back.

"I may not know why I am here," he explained to her, kindly, "but I know that I need to find my way back. You and I are friends, where I come from," he smiled, "and I know how clever, trust-worthy and inventive you are. Will you come with me now?" he asked, an almost pleading look in his eyes, "Help me look for my sleigh and help me find my way home?"

"Of course," she nodded with a warm smile, "I'll do anything I can to help you. That's why I'm here after all, although I didn't quite imagine it would be like this! The others know already that you are here so if they come looking for me and find us both gone then they will know that I have gone with you."

"We'll be back before dinner time," Nicholai promised her, "No one will even miss us. I am still feeling quite weak from the accident and don't want to stray too far from here but besides that," he grinned, "no way am I going to pass up the chance to enjoy one of my mother's fabulous dinners!"

Seven

The agreement reached between them, Nicholai climbed up onto the horse and held out his hand to help the elf up in front of him so that they could share the saddle. The low gate of the courtyard designed to stop animals from the fields wandering in rather than as any sort of security measure, was standing open as it often did during the day to allow the easy coming and going of guests, deliveries and other visitors.

Although she had clearly been very good at taking care of the animal, Nicholai could tell that the small elf was not comfortable riding a horse and realised that this was probably the first time she had done so. Other than their occasional forays into the forest around the cave entrance and, in more recent years, trips to the Pieten village less than half a day's walk from their own home, the elves did not leave the cave system. Nicholai had to admit he was surprised that they had come this far away to watch over his younger self but he supposed that it answered his question about how they had been able to react so quickly when Annalina got caught in the storm.

To comfort her and make her feel safe, Nicholai put one arm around her waist from behind, holding her in place, and took the reins with his other hand. He had done the same for Annalina when they were children as, although less than two years her senior, he had always felt very protective of her and considered himself responsible for her safety. It seemed strange to Nicholai that his travelling companion, who, from her perspective, had only just met him, looked no different from the elf that he knew and had been friends with for three centuries. Yet, he supposed, that was the irony of immortality. Had he met her five, eight or even twenty centuries before now, she would not have looked any different and if he now were to meet his own self from a further future, he knew that he would not have changed.

The only member of the party who did not seem to be in any way troubled by what was going on was Sleipnir. It seemed not to bother him that the Nicholai who now rode him was twice the size and three times as heavy as the boy he was used to, or that the two shared very few physical characteristics in common. He recognised this grown Nicholai from the future as his master, the same person as the young boy who was his usual rider, and that was all that mattered to him.

"What exactly are we looking for?" the elf asked after they had been riding for almost an hour, "Some sort of hole in time that you might have fallen through?"

"No." Nicholai chuckled, "I'm trying to find my sleigh. I know I must have been riding it when whatever it was happened to me, although I still can't remember exactly what that was. I'm hoping that it would have come through with me and that it might give me some sort of clue as to what happened. If I know how I got here then I might be able to find my way back."

"But if you're eternal like us," the elf asked, "couldn't you just wait? You won't get any older, however long you have to wait to get back to your own time. Couldn't you find somewhere to settle and just wait until enough time had passed then come back home, apparently minutes after you left?" Nicholai could not deny that the thought had crossed his mind but he had found it utterly unpalatable.

"Absolutely not." he informed the elf, firmly but not unkindly, "That would mean being apart from her for another three centuries. We were apart before for only a few decades and it felt like an eternity. To be separated again for so long would be more than I could handle. I already miss her more than I can say and it was only a few days ago I saw her. I understand your thinking but no, that's not an option. Something happened to bring me here; it must be also possible for me to get back." The elf nodded quietly but said nothing for a few minutes before changing the subject.

"In my time," she told him, "we have only just started working on your sleigh. They say it will take twenty years or more to be ready. I've not been working on it myself but I've enjoyed going and watching some of the others working on it. It's amazing to see something emerge out of a huge, solid lump of wood like that. It's like the sleigh was always inside and they're just cleaning off the other wood that has stuck to it. Does that sound like a strange thing to say?"

"Not at all." Nicholai assured her, "I know exactly what you mean. I've ridden in and on plenty of carts and carriages but I've never known anything quite like it. It feels like its still alive somehow, like growing as a tree was just its infancy and now it has become what it was always supposed to be. A bit like when a caterpillar becomes a butterfly. I'd always thought that a tree died when it fell and that anything built from it would simply be dead wood but that really isn't the case with the sleigh but then," he grinned, "it wasn't just any old tree to begin with, was it? Tell me," he asked, "what does it look like in your time?"

"Like a simple toy, I suppose." the elf mused, "All that's been done so far is the basic shape has been cut out and hollowed. It's all very rough and there's no carving or anything like that. It's recognisable as a sleigh but nothing that special. It's really a larger version of a toy sleigh a father might whittle from a piece for fallen wood for his son or daughter. I've seen in the book how it will look when it's finished and I'm sure it will be amazingly beautiful! The paintings, I'm sure, cannot really do it justice even if they are created by magic."

"Then I hope we do find it," Nicholai gave her tummy a little affectionate squeeze with his arm, "and that you get a chance to see it because it really is more beautiful than you could ever imagine."

"How do you guide it?" the elf asked, hoping that she already knew the answer, "I know it should be able to rise off the ground by itself but it will still need to be pulled."

"Reindeer!" Nicholai grinned broadly, "Eight magnificent, flying reindeer! Annalina told me how she discovered them in the forest when she was still little, shortly after she came to live with you, and named them."

"That worked then?" grinned the elf, "I knew that when the sleigh was finished it was intended that the reindeer who had eaten the fruit of the tree while it was still standing should pull it but they always seemed so wild, I never really believed they'd be persuaded to do it!"

"Ah well my Annalina has quite a way with wild beasts! After all," he chuckled, "she managed to tame me!"

"Shh!" the elf threw up her hand and Nicholai brought the horse to a gentle stop.

"What is it?" he leant forward and whispered softly, knowing that his friend must have spotted something. Living for countless centuries in the half-light of the caves had not only resulted in the elves eyes growing larger than those of modern humans but had made them sharper in the daylight. Although Nicholai's own eyesight had improved in the time that he had been with them, also thanks to the healing and rejuvenating effects of the fruit juice he and Annalina had drank at their wedding, he knew that his eyes were no match for those of an elf and was not at all surprised that she had noticed something he had not.

"Over there!" pointed the elf in equally hushed tones. Looking in the direction indicated by her finger, Nicholai saw a flash of red. As he quickly focussed in the right area, he saw that it was his younger self being led by the hand by his sweetheart.

Worried that Sleipnir would recognise his young master and want to go to him or call out and betray their presence, Nicholai suggested that they should follow on foot. He reasoned that it would be better to follow the young couple and continue searching for the sleigh later rather than risk running into them and having to explain what they were doing there, especially riding young Nicholai's horse. While the youngster had been very accepting of the strange visitor who appeared to have come out of nowhere, if he were to see him in the forest with his horse and in the company of a stable girl he might assume that they were working together to rob his family and run back to the house to warn them. Also, Nicholai didn't want to disturb his younger self and Annalina in what he knew would be one of their last few days together before their separation.

Hopping down from the horse, he held out his hand to help down the elf who only narrowly avoided falling on her face. As she dusted herself off, Nicholai tied Sleipnir to a tree and fished a small treat for him out of his pocket.

"Come on!" his small friend urged in a quiet but urgent tone, "We don't want them to get too far ahead or we might lose sight of them." Allowing the elf with her superior vision to go ahead, Nicholai followed as they tracked the young couple through the forest, taking care to stay far enough away so as not to be noticed but close enough to be sure to keep them in sight.

"Oh dear!" the elf came to a sudden stop, almost causing Nicholai to trip over her.

"What is it?" Nicholai asked, before looking up and seeing exactly what the problem was. Up ahead, the children were clambering over a large, dark shape which, less than a second later, Nicholai recognised as his sleigh. "Oh dear." he observed, as much to himself as to the elf, "It looks as if things just got a whole lot more complicated!"

Eight

"How much further?" the dark-haired young boy asked as Annalina tugged at his hand, urging him to follow her, "My legs are starting to get tired! Can we at least slow down a bit?"

"Oh yes, I forgot," she turned and stuck her tongue out at him, "You're really old!" Two years is a long time when you are a child and Annalina loved to tease Nicholai about being such an old man.

"That's right!" he stood, trying to catch his breath and steady his heartbeat, "And you never seem to get tired at all!"

"That's because I'm special!" she grinned at him.

"Indeed you are!" he chuckled, pulling her forward with his hands on her shoulders and kissing her. "But seriously," he pushed a lock of hair out of her face; "if we're not going to be there soon then I'm going to need to take a little break."

"Well we're stood still now aren't we?" Annalina teased, "Isn't that enough of a break for you?" The look on her beloved's face seemed genuinely worried so she decided not to be too mean to him this time. "No, really," she assured him, "it's just behind those trees over there."

Up until that point on their journey, the young couple had been holding hands but now the forest was getting considerably thicker and they found that it just wasn't practical. With nearly every step they had to push low-hanging branches out the way or take exaggeratedly large steps to avoid catching their clothing on brambles and other low-lying creepers.

"There!" Annalina pointed excitedly as she pulled back the last branch between her and her target, "Over there! See it?" So excited was she that she let the branch go, not realising just how close behind her Nicholai was standing. The poor boy let out a yelp as it swung back with considerable force and slapped him around the face. "Oh I'm sorry!" she giggled, not looking very sorry at all, "I didn't know you were right there. Are you all right?"

"I think so!" he exclaimed, chuckling as he saw the funny side of the incident, "I'll let you know if I have any..." he broke off as he saw where she was pointing, "What is that?"

"I'm not sure," Annalina frowned a little as she moved into the small clearing where the large object was sat, partially buried, "It looks like a sleigh but how could it have got into the middle of the forest," she looked around at the dense woodland which appeared to be utterly undisturbed. The only signs of any kind of disturbance were a few broken branches, almost as if the object had fallen from the sky, crashing through the canopy of trees as it did so but surely that was impossible. "Anyway," she turned to Nicholai, "there's no snow, hasn't been for weeks. How could it have got here?"

"I don't know." Nicholai began running his hands over the exposed edge. Whatever it was, it seemed to be made from dark, polished hard-wood with intricate carvings over it, like the fine wardrobes in his parents' bedroom. It certainly did look like some sort of sleigh or coach but far grander than any he had seen before. "What seems stranger to me," he observed, "is that it looks like somebody tried to bury it. Why would anyone do that?"

"Maybe they stole it," Annalina suggested, "and wanted to hide it here so they could come back for it later. Maybe they tried covering it with mud and that sort of thing so no one else could see it?"

"Seems a very strange thing to do." Nicholai mused. "After all, if they'd stolen it and didn't want anyone to recognise it they could just put it on the back of a bigger cart and cover it over with sacking. Leaving it here buried makes no sense – it could spoil the lovely finish on this wood and, anyway, anyone coming across it here would still think it was mighty strange to see a big mound of freshly-dug earth in the middle of the woods!"

"What I don't understand," remarked Annalina, studying the exposed carvings and tracing the outline of one of the strange little figures with the tip of her finger, "is why, if they were going to bury it, would they stop half way like this? Besides, it's pointing downwards like they dug a hole and pushed the front in then started building up the earth around it."

"You said you saw it before," Nicholai reminded her, "earlier this morning? Might you have disturbed whoever it was while they were burying it so they ran away?"

"I'd have heard them." Annalina replied confidently, "I'm sure I would have. It was ever so quiet. All I heard while I was here," she thought hard to make sure she was remembering the details correctly, "was something up in the trees, moving around the branches. It sounded a bit like a squirrel but heavier, almost like there was a cat up there. I couldn't see anything when I looked and I didn't think too much about it. It was so quiet, I expect any noise would have sounded a lot louder than it really was."

"Very strange." Nicholai said again, continuing to study the carving. Pushing aside some of the loose earth, he noticed something else strange. The wood got noticeably darker as he cleared away the debris and the finish more course. After a few moments' exploration, his hand slid over a section that was very rough and brittle, seeming to crumble under his touch. Feeling as if he were a little closer to solving the mystery, he began to scoop the earth away with both hands until enough of the object beneath had been revealed to confirm his suspicions.

"Look!" he pointed, beckoning Annalina over with his other hand, "It's been burned. It's like charcoal here." He broke off a small piece between finger and thumb to show how brittle it was. "Looks like whoever left it here tried to burn it and, when that didn't work, they tried burying it instead."

"Or maybe it caught fire," Annalina suggested, "and they threw the dirt over it to put the fire out?"

"If that was the case," Nicholai stroked his chin, "I would have thought they'd have gone for help then come back to retrieve it. Either way, they certainly wouldn't just leave it here like this. If they were bothered enough about it to want to put out the fire then surely they wouldn't just abandon it like this?"

"What I still don't understand," Annalina observed, scrambling up the pile of dry dirt and debris from the forest floor in order to get inside the sleigh and see how the burned section looked from the inside, "is how it got here in the first place! There's simply no path for it to have got here."

"Maybe it got left here a long time ago?" Nicholai suggested, "Maybe there was a path here once and the forest has grown back around it."

"I don't think so," Annalina brushed more of the dirt away and looked closely at the wood. "If it had been here a long time then it would look old. It would be dirty and have things growing on it. Look," she reached over and pointed out to Nicholai how clean and well-maintained the wood appeared under the soil, apart from the fire-damaged areas, "this is new. Or at least it's been well looked after. It can only have been here a few days at most. Anyway," she stood up on the seat of the sleigh and kicked at the debris covering the front half, "this soil is all recently churned up. If it had been here any amount of time it would be all solid but it's not."

"Then perhaps someone's been building it, out here in the forest where no one would see what they were doing." Nicholai ventured another theory, "But then something happened to make it catch fire, maybe they had a camping stove or something, and they either put the fire out with the soil or got upset and decided to bury it as it was ruined."

"Why would anyone build a sleigh in the middle of the forest?" Annalina raised an eyebrow, suggesting that she found this theory the most implausible of all that had been put forward so far. "What would be the point of building something like this if you'd never be able to get it out? Look," she reached out and touched the trunk of a nearby tree to demonstrate how close it was, "there's not even room to attach any horses to pull it out with."

"I guess it must just have fallen from the sky then!" Nicholai stuck out his tongue, feeling a little foolish but managing to cover it well. Annalina was, by now, climbing all over the half-submerged sleigh, trying to work out just how big it was and how bad the damage was. Trying to work out whether any of it had actually been burned away or if the wood was simply scorched.

"Hey!" she called to Nicholai, on her hands and knees caring nothing for the state her clothes would be in by the time she got home. "Come and look at this!"

Taking his coat off so as not to risk tearing it, Nicholai folded it fairly neatly and laid it over one of the cleaner parts of the mysterious sleigh then, shivering a little in only his shirt but knowing he would soon warm up once he started climbing about and exploring, he heaved himself up onto the mound of dirt and tried to see what Annalina was pointing at. She was kneeling on the polished wood floor of the sleigh, in front of the bench which served as a seat and looking down into space where the rider or riders would put their feet. It was mostly filled with soil, leaves and twigs although there was one fairly large branch which looked as if it had been ripped from one of the trees above and dropped in there.

"What am I supposed to see?" Nicholai got down on his hands and knees beside her, as a slight angle so as not to slide down the tilting floor.

"There!" Annalina pointed, "Look under the branch."

Looking where her finger pointed, Nicholai suddenly realised what she had seen. Under the branch was a gap in the mud, as if something had tunnelled in. It reminded him of the entrance to a badger set like the one Joseph had shown him in the summer time. On the polished wooden floor in front of it, he saw with surprise, were deep scratches, like claw marks, as if something had crawled out from the makeshift tunnel, dragging itself up the incline with its claws.

"Be careful!" Nicholai warned, as Annalina leaned her head into the darkness to try to see what was inside, "What if something's still in there?"

"I don't think this was something tunnelling in." she explained, "If an animal wanted to make a burrow or something they have done it underneath where it's safer and the earth is all nicely churned up. I think whatever made this hole got stuck in there where the mud was thrown over it and had to tunnel its way out."

"I still think you should be careful!" cautioned Nicholai as Annalina stood, grabbed his coat from where he had left it and began rummaging in the pockets, pulling out various lengths of string, a penknife, three pine cones, two small stones which he had picked up because of their interesting pattern and various unidentifiable objects which had probably once been part of something else, before finally finding what she was looking for. A small box of matches.

Crouching down again with her head at the opening of the tunnel, she struck a match and reached down into the darkness, peering closely to see if there might be any other evidence of what had been down there before the match burned down almost to her fingers and she had to drop it. Luckily, the dry earth it fell onto snuffed it out quite effectively and she did not add to the damage already done to the beautiful carving by the original fire.

"What if whatever it was had gone back down there?" Nicholai chastised her, "You know how dangerous animals can be when they're scared, especially if you startle them!"

"I knew there was nothing alive down there." she informed him confidently, "If there had been, I'd have been able to hear it breathing. Anyway," she beamed at him, "You're here! And I know nothing bad can happen to me while you're around!"

"So," Nicholai asked, blushing a little but gladdened by her absolute faith in him, "what did you see down there?"

"I'm not sure," Annalina furrowed her brow, "it looked like bright pieces of cloth, mostly torn up, but I don't know what those would be doing down there."

"Some birds collect scraps to make their nests with," Nicholai mused, sitting up and resting his back against the seat behind, his knees bent and his feet against the earthy bank inside the sleigh, "but I've never heard of badgers or rabbits doing anything like that."

"Maybe it was something in the sleigh?" she suggested, "And whatever got stuck in here tore it up while they were trying to get out."

"Possibly." Nicholai scratched the top of his head, "Help me move this stuff then we can get a proper look. I want to see if there are any more scratches too."

Between them, they managed to shift the bulk of the loose soil and forest debris out of the sleigh, lifting it and dumping it over the sides. By the time they had removed all but the last traces which clung to the polished wood, they were both hot and filthy.

Kneeling down, Nicholai picked up and examined the scraps of cloth that Annalina had seen by the light of the match. Upon closer inspection, they actually appeared to be items of clothing, brightly coloured and very small. Possibly for an infant but more like the kind of clothing that would be made for a doll of some kind.

"How strange!" Annalina took a yellow shirt from Nicholai and turned it over in her hands. "See all these rips? And the big one on the back? It looks like whatever, or whoever was down here got caught on something on their way up and the shirt got torn so they ripped the rest of it off to get away more easily."

"Oh and look here!" Nicholai pointed at the kick-plate at the back of the recessed space where the riders' feet would go if they stretched out their legs. "There's more scratches on the back. It's like when they got trapped they didn't know where they were so just started clawing all around until something gave way and they were able to tunnel out. They must have been terrified!"

"How many of them do you think there were?" Annalina asked, starting to feel very sorry for whatever creatures it was that had been trapped when the sleigh had been covered.

"It looks like there's two sets of clothes here," Nicholai was picking through the brightly-coloured rags, trying to piece them together, "so probably there were two of them. I wonder what they are?"

"Well these clothes are only really big enough for babies," Annalina held up the tattered shirt, "but babies don't have claws! And anyway, they wouldn't have known what to do."

"Must be an animal of some kind," Nicholai mused, "but why would animals be wearing clothes?"

"I did see a man in the market once," Annalina remembered, "he was playing the accordion and had a little monkey with him that sat on his shoulder and collected coins from the audience in a little bowl. He was wearing a funny little waistcoat and hat so maybe it's something like that?"

"Hmm," Nicholai studied the clothes again, "Too small for a person but too big for any monkey I've seen. It really is a mystery!"

Nine

"What's wrong?" the elf asked, in hushed tones although she was not entirely sure why. "Why did you stop?" Nicholai held his finger up to his lips to motion to her to stay quiet then guided her around in front of him and pulled the branches back a little so that she'd be able to see what he had seen.

Curiously, she peered at what lay ahead, intrigued to know what had caused Nicholai to stop dead in his tracks and take a step backwards, almost tripping over her in the process.

There was no mistaking the object in the clearing. Even though she had only ever seen it in its crude, incomplete form and illustrations of how it was destined to look when completed, the half-submerged object was obviously the sleigh, carved in a single piece from the wood of the life-giving tree which, in her time, had only fallen a few short years before, at the time when, she now understood, the intended rider of the sleigh had been born.

While it was intriguing to see this fabled vehicle she had dreamed so often of seeing, she realised instantly why Nicholai had been alarmed. Clambering over the sleigh and investigating it with great interest were the young Annalina and Nicholai, decades before they were supposed to see it.

"What should we do?" she asked, looking up at the adult Nicholai with worried eyes.

"We should wait for now," he cautioned her, "stay out of sight. Hopefully they won't understand what it is." What puzzled him most about what he was seeing, he did not tell the elf for fear of worrying and confusing her further, was that while he remembered meeting the old man he now knew to be his adult self around this time, he had no memory of the sleigh. Could it actually be that time was being altered before his eyes? But surely, he thought, if that were the case then his memories would be altered too?

As he watched, he saw his younger self holding up the tattered clothing of the Pieten – clothing that had been made as a gift by the elves for the hairy little wild men who had no need of it but enjoyed it all the same. This meant, he realised, that there must have been at least one of them in the sleigh with him. Hitting himself on the forehead, he wondered why he had not thought of this before.

In the early days of his gift-giving expeditions, the homes he had delivered to had usually been easily accessible through an unlocked door or window. Some of the poorer homes didn't even have a door as such, just a heavy curtain over the entrance to block out the draught. Even when there was a lock of sorts in place, it tended to be a simple latch, more to stop the door swinging open on its own than as any measure of security, easy to open from the outside with a slim-bladed knife, but in more recent years as the world had changed with people becoming more fearful for their safety and most homes now having things within them that others would want to steal, gaining access to the houses had become more and more of a challenge.

With every year, his fame and reputation grew. Knowing that people were becoming curious about the identity of the annual gift-giver, he and Annalina had decided to release small snippets of information in the form of poems or songs and, for a number of years, in the days running up to his delivery, Nicholai had flown the sleigh through remote but sparsely populated areas, allowing some children to see him or entering towns and villages and talking to the children he met there, telling them the stories he had always so enjoyed sharing on his travels and hinting to them about his true identity, although always being careful to leave just enough ambiguity to make them wonder whether he was for real or not.

Some strange side-effects had resulted from these visits. Knowing no other name, Nicholai had always continued to introduce himself as he had in his mortal life as Nicholai, son of Claus. His accent, strange to many, had caused confusion amongst some children who confused "son of" with their word for holy or good, "Sancte". As this seemed to fit so well with their impressions of the mysterious man who brought them gifts every year, they never questioned it, simply referring to the man amongst themselves as Sancte Claus, which in time became corrupted to Santa Claus and people began to believe this was his proper, given name.

His first name, however, was not forgotten, although in the passing on it had become confused with the more common Nicholas which in turn led to a greater confusion which Nicholai himself found rather embarrassing but which Annalina thought was the funniest thing ever. Given that Sancte could be a title for a revered Saint or holy man, people began to think of him as Nicholas, Saint Claus or simply as Saint Nicholas or Saint Claus, creating a great confusion with a great man from the East who had lived nearly ten centuries before Nicholai's birth.

People began to say that the annual gift-giver was indeed Saint Nicholas of Myra, returned from Heaven to continue his charitable work for which he had become famous in the years immediately following his life. So close was the association that some even considered "Saint Nick" to be interchangeable with the adopted title of

Santa Claus. Humbled by the association in the public imagination, Nicholai had done his best to find out as much as he could about the life and work of the holy man, including several volumes of history and legend related to him in the vast library that he and Annalina had been building since his arrival in the caves so very many years ago.

As homes had become less accessible, the legends had granted Nicholai the ability to enter houses through magical means, an ability he did not in fact possess, but those who relied on his annual visits did not consider that he would have a problem delivering his gifts. To get around this problem, Nicholai had begun taking one or two of the Pieten with him as they were able to scrabble down the chimneys and then open the doors from inside before locking the door behind him and leaving the property the same way they had got in, making use of their strong, sharp claws to climb the sooty brickwork. Possibly due to the deposits of soot left by their visits, people had come to associate chimneys with Nicholai's visits, suggesting that he himself was somehow able to climb down them with his sack of gifts and leave the same way as if transformed to smoke.

It had become customary to either hang socks on the mantelpiece, or leave a pair of shoes by the hearth to be filled with small gifts and other treats. Nicholai always looked fondly upon these as it reminded him of his childhood when he and Annalina would often return from their adventures with soaking wet, muddy feet and their socks, stockings and shoes would have to be dried out by the fire on practically a nightly basis.

How, he wondered to himself, cursing his amnesia-fogged brain, could he have forgotten that he had been travelling with Pieten when he had been hurled back into his own past? Desperately, he wondered what had become of them. Although he knew that, like him, the Pieten could not actually be killed, he still feared for them as he also knew that they were more than capable of suffering grave injury and pain. Even if you would eventually heal with no evidence of the injury, having every bone in your body smashed by a crash-landing would still be unbelievably painful. So painful, in fact, that you may wish that you could die rather than be forced to live through such agony.

Taking a few deep breaths to calm himself, Nicholai tried to think rationally about the situation. What the children were holding up and discussing between them were tattered clothes, not broken bodies. He knew Annalina and his younger self well enough to know that, had there been any sign of a wounded creature, whether they recognised it as a type of person or simply considered it an animal, they would focus on helping them and trying to relieve their suffering rather than investigating the remnants of their clothing. Also, unless they had torn them off in fear and panic at the time of the accident, the rags probably meant that the Pieten had got away, gone into hiding somewhere in the forest, leaving behind the loose-fitting clothes that got caught on some debris or others.

As he pondered the fate of his diminutive companions, it occurred to Nicholai that, since the reindeer and he himself seemed to be unharmed by the incident, aside from the disorientation and slight memory loss, then the Pieten were probably fine too. He wasn't sure if they would realise who the children currently clambering over and exploring the sleigh were. Even if they did, they would be wise enough to understand that the young folk would not recognise them so would stay out of sight until the youngsters had gone.

Looking at his majestic vehicle, half buried in the mud, Nicholai suddenly had a flashback, as if the sight had prompted one of the lost memories to jump to the surface of his consciousness. He saw himself falling, tumbling like an acrobat as he did so to try to slow his descent or at least prevent himself from hitting the ground like a dropped rock. Closing his eyes, Nicholai could picture the scene now very clearly. He was soaked to the skin, the rain still lashing down around him as he fell. Below him, he could see trees, illuminated for split-seconds at a time by the lightning. The rushing of the wind in his ears all but blocked out the crashes of thunder that seemed to explode around him.

In his mind's eye, Nicholai saw himself crashing into the trees, the branches breaking his fall, before hitting the ground with an impact that was still enough to knock the wind from him but could still have proved fatal to a mortal man. Staggering to his feet, feeling the cuts and scrapes on his face and the broken ribs inside his chest already starting to heal, Nicholai had wandered through the forest that seemed so familiar yet he was not sure why. He walked instinctively, as if sure of his path although he had no real idea of where he was heading. Emerging from the forest into a vast, open meadow, he saw that the storm had already passed on and the unseasonably warm breeze began to dry his sodden clothes and hair.

As he approached the brow of a slight hill, he had realised where he was. The building ahead was his parents' house, the place where he had spent his childhood. Looking back now, Nicholai wondered how he could have missed the fact that the building no longer existed in that form and that, as far as he knew, nobody there would know or recognise him but, back in the moment, disoriented and scared by his fall from so high in the sky, he had simply seen it as a place of safety, somewhere he could go to recover and be looked after.

Rubbing his sore but no longer broken ribs, he trudged forward towards the familiar gate. The gates had been locked as they so often were at night but this had not bothered him too much. As a boy, he had often stayed out past dark, exploring and playing in the forest, and had become very adept at climbing over the gates. While it was a little harder with his increased size and bruised, aching body, he was still able to make his way over. His head still spinning and his body drained from having healed the wounds from the crash, he had only managed to walk half way across the courtyard before he collapsed and that is where his younger self had found him several hours later.

"We should be getting back," the young Nicholai suggested to his little sweetheart, the sound of his voice grabbing his older elf's attention and snapping out of his daydreams of forgotten memories and back into the moment, "I think it's going to start snowing soon and I don't want to get caught out in it. Anyway," he grinned, "I'm getting hungry and I'm sure Mama was baking a cake! You wouldn't want to miss that, would you?"

"No," Annalina giggled, "I wouldn't want to miss cake! But what are we going to do about this? We can't just leave it here."

"We'll tell Joseph about it later," the boy suggested, running his fingers through his thick, black hair, "He'll know what to do. He always knows what to do about stuff like this."

"But what if it does snow?" insisted Annalina, "It will get covered up and we won't be able to find it again."

"Ah but if we can't find it," Nicholai chuckled, "then nobody else will be able to either so it won't be going anywhere. Once the snow melts we'll come back and show Joseph. If it doesn't snow later after all, then we can just come back tonight!"

"That's true!" Annalina agreed with another giggle, "Besides, I don't think anyone would be able to move it even if they found it. Not without two or even four very big horses at least. I think it should be pretty safe." Nicholai jumped down to the ground and held up his arms to help Annalina. He caught her as she jumped but had not been quite expecting how hard she was going to hit him so fell over backwards onto the soft, churched up earth, his little sweetheart on top of him and giggling hysterically. "Are you okay?" she asked, once she had managed to get her breath back, "I didn't mean to knock you over!"

"Yes you did!" he teased, "But I'm fine. It's a good job I was here to catch you or you'd have a face full of mud right now!"

"I knew you'd catch me," she leant forward and kissed him sweetly, "you're always there to catch me when I fall. I know I'll always be safe with you. When you're around, nothing bad could happen to me! Now come on!" she leapt up and held out her hand to help her somewhat muddy friend to his feet, "Let's go and see if that cake you mentioned is ready yet!"

Observing from his safe distance, the much older Nicholai at first stood smiling warmly at the touching scene, remembering those happy, carefree days of his childhood when his world had been small and his future seemed clear. But then, all of a sudden, he felt a sickening lurch in his stomach as the revelation hit him.

That terrible day, the day that his beloved had been taken from him and his life was changed forever, that was today. The carefree young couple who had just walked hand in hand away from the sleigh, their heads filled with nothing but love and cake, would not make it home together before the snow hit.

"What is it?" the little dark-haired elf tugged on his hand, seeing the tears rolling down his cheeks and soaking into his thick white beard.

"Today..." he replied through his tears, struggling to get the words out, "Today is the day that she was taken from me. Today is the day that she dies."

Ten

"It's too early to go home just yet." Annalina observed, a cheeky smile on her freckled face, "I think we should play a game first.

"What sort of game?" Nicholai asked, torn between the desire to keep his impish sweetheart happy and his desire for the cake he knew would be waiting for them when they got home.

"Hide and seek!" grinned Annalina. It was by far her favourite game and, while she was perfectly capable of staying hidden for hours if she chose to, when playing with the other local children, she always made sure that Nicholai was able to find her quite easily when it was just the two of them together. This did not, however, stop him from teasing her by loudly proclaiming, when he knew that she was within ear-shot that he would never be able to find her and that he would have to tell her parents that she was gone forever.

"I suppose you will be hiding?" He asked with a chuckle, knowing the answer already. Annalina nodded, her grin spreading ever wider. "And what prize do I get if I manage to find you?"

"A kiss!"

"A kiss?" Nicholai teased, "What's one of those?"

Giggling, Annalina bounced forward onto the tips of her toes and kissed him noisily on the cheek.

"If you find me," she promised him, "you can have another of those. If you can find me quickly enough," her eyes sparkled, "then you can have two!" With that, she ran off into the distance, ignoring the first flakes of snow that were starting to fall around her.

Somewhat pensively, Nicholai looked up at the darkening sky as he began to count slowly back from one hundred. Before he had reached twenty, the snow had begun to fall more heavily. Breaking off his count, he decided that it was more important to find Annalina and to make sure she got home safely before the snow blocked their path which, he knew, could well happen, especially as far away from either of their homes as they were.

Knowing that she would most likely want to be found, Nicholai began to run in the direction Annalina had gone, hoping to catch up with her but he could not see her. She must already have found herself a hiding place. A sense of cold dread formed in the pit of Nicholai's stomach and began to rise, becoming more and more urgent as it made its way up through his body, causing his heart to beat rapidly in panic before erupting from his throat as a desperate cry. Already the snow-storm had become so thick and heavy that he could not see beyond the end of his nose as anything more than dark, abstract shadows.

Blindly, Nicholai continued to run towards where he had last seen Annalina, calling out to her all the time but realising that it was very unlikely she would be able to hear him. The snow was accompanied by a violent wind which seemed to snatch the words from his mouth as soon as he had uttered them.

Still desperately searching through the blizzard for his beloved, looking as hard as he could for any hint of her red cloak against the white snow but seeing none, the panicked boy did not see the looming shape of a horse and rider on the horizon, watching him in his desperation and despair.

Eleven

"I wonder if..." Nicholai broke off, seeing a large flake of snow settle on his thick, white beard. Looking up to the sky, he saw more flakes beginning to fall. The children had run off excitedly together, their hearts filled with nothing but love for each other and their minds filled with excitement and expectations about one of Nicholai's mother's famous cakes. But Nicholai knew that it was a cake they would never get to sample, at least not together. He thought back to that terrible night, ever so many years ago.

After insisting that there was no more they could do to find Annalina, his father had almost had to drag him back inside the house and hold him as they sat by the fire to dry. Nicholai had wanted to go back out to continue the search but they snow had been falling more thickly and heavily than ever and his father had kindly but firmly told him that all that would be achieved if he were to go back out looking for her would be that he would be lost too. Everyone had sworn to him that it was not his fault and that there was nothing else he could have done but his heart told him otherwise. The thought of the last words he had just heard from the fresh-faced, vibrant little girl, addressed to his younger self, stung him like a shard of ice through his heart.

"I let her down." he spoke softly, as much to himself as to the small elf who stood by his side, gripping his hand tightly, "She trusted me. She said that nothing bad could happen to her while I was around but I failed her."

"I wouldn't be so sure about that." the elf smiled up at him, saddened by the bitter tears she saw in his eyes but determined to help him see the role of fate in the situation. "You're here now, aren't you? Do you think that this is an accident?"

"It was." Nicholai replied, confused. "The storm, the lightning. It must be something to do with the properties of the wood which, I'm sure, you know all about. In my own time, the time I was living in before the storm, people have learned to generate and harness lightning-like power; it's how the towns and cities have been able to grow as large as they have. When the lightning hit the sleigh it must have over-loaded it with power and caused its ability to freeze time around it to work a little too well so that it actually rewound time."

"A freak accident that happened to bring you back to the place you grew up at the exact time she went missing and you took your first steps on the path to becoming the man you are now? Yes," the elf sniggered, "I'm sure it was a total coincidence."

"What are you saying?"

"The snow has begun to fall, right?" Nicholai nodded, wondering where the elf's explanation was leading, "And how many elves do you see around here?"

"Just you," Nicholai admitted, "but there could be others around or they could be on their way here."

"No," giggled the elf, amused by how slow on the uptake Nicholai appeared to be being, "I can assure you there are no others around and they are not on their way. Your home is less than an hour's walk from here and you know that she never made it to the end of that journey. How long do you suppose a little girl can survive out there, buried by snow?"

"I don't know." Nicholai looked away, hating the thought, "Two hours perhaps, maybe three, but not much longer."

"And you know the caves are far more than three hours' journey from here?" he nodded again, "Then do you not suppose," she grinned broadly, "that there might be a reason that you are here and that you and I might have something very significant to do with what happens next?"

"You mean...?"

"I do mean! Come on!" she tugged on his hand, urging him to move, "We need to stay close behind them. You know what's about to happen but you didn't see exactly where she went, you couldn't have done! If we follow quickly, we should be able to catch them up but we need to make sure we stay out of sight."

To save time and to avoid being slowed down by her small legs, Nicholai picked up the elf and swung her on Sleipnir's back then led the horse as quickly as he could back to the edge of the wooded area. Once out in the open, he could see two small figures in the distance, Annalina made easy to spot by her distinctive red cloak. The young sweethearts did not seem to be in any particular hurry, which Nicholai was grateful for as it meant that they had not got too far ahead of him, and were laughing and teasing each other as they walked, oblivious to the lightly-falling snow which was so much a part of their day-to-day lives at this time of year that they barely noticed it.

Now that he was out in the open, Nicholai climbed up onto Sleipnir's back behind the elf and put a protective arm around her middle as he had done before. He moved the obedient horse forward only a few steps at a time, taking care to keep the children in sight but staying far enough away that they would be unlikely to notice him.

Already the snow was starting to fall heavier more quickly.

The heavier the snow became, the closer Nicholai found he had to stay to the pair to keep them in sight. It took every ounce of self-restraint he could muster not to simply ride up to them and offer them a ride back to the house on his horse; or rather the horse that he had borrowed from his younger self, but he knew that he could not do that because that is not what happened. He was not altering the past, merely participating in it as his childhood memories told him he always had.

The snow was now so heavy he could barely see through it. Young Annalina and Nicholai seemed to have been parted. From atop the horse, he could see them both but it was clear that they could not see each other. With a sickening lurch in his stomach and his tears streaking his face and soaking his beard, Nicholai saw Annalina vanish from sight. She had fallen. This was the moment that he had lost her.

Wishing that he could help but knowing that he mustn't, Nicholai watched the young boy he had once been searching desperately for his lost love. Knowing that he had only searched for a few minutes before rushing off to get help, Nicholai held himself back and waited. Soon enough, he saw the panicked little boy running off into the distance and, knowing that there was no time to waste, urged Sleipnir forward through the snow.

As they galloped, the elf wound her hands into the magnificent beast's mane and gripped tightly, afraid of falling off into the snow at high speed. As he urged the horse forward, Nicholai was grateful for how well trained his childhood companion was, how he did not seemed bothered by the snow yet would know instinctively to stop before running over any dangerous ledges or slopes. Quickly, they reached the spot where he had last seen Annalina. After bringing Sleipnir to a stop by tugging on the reins, Nicholai jumped down and helped the elf to the ground then they both began searching for the missing girl.

Understanding that she would be unconscious by now, Nicholai did not try calling for her. Instead he focussed on what he knew about Annalina and tried to work out what she would do in the circumstances. He knew she had to be somewhere towards the bottom of the slope. A sensible girl who had always lived in this relatively harsh environment, she would have known to take shelter. There were no trees anywhere nearby but there were several large rocks, rapidly being covered by the snow. He was sure that he would find her behind one of these.

Calling a quick explanation and suggestion for where to look to the elf, he began to run as fast as he could through the ever-deepening snow, plunging his hands down through the icy white powder, hoping desperately to feel either skin or fabric, anything other than long grass or rubble. Beneath the third rock he came to, he felt her thick, woollen cloak. With a shout to the elf, calling for her to come help, Nicholai sank to his knees and began to shovel the snow out of the way with his hands until he was able to pull out the small, cold little body, wrapped in the thick red cloak which had made her so easy to keep track of in the snow. Cradling her in his arms and pulling down her hood as the snow continued to fall around them, Nicholai feared that he may already be too late but the very faint wisps of breath condensing in the frigid air told him that the fragile spark of life still remained within her.

Fearing that the soaking wool of her cloak would cling to her and force the deadly chill within her, Nicholai quickly removed his own heavy coat, pulled off Annalina's cloak and wrapped her in his own coat. The cold bit into his skin beneath his thin shirt but he knew that it could not hurt him. Not that he cared about his own safety at that moment. Even if he had not been immortal and impervious to any lasting damage, he would still have done whatever he possibly could to keep Annalina safe. He had spent his life believing that he had failed her at the time she needed him most. Now he had been given a chance to put that right and he was determined not to waste it.

Twelve

"I could take her back home, to her parents." Nicholai suggested, sitting in the snow with Annalina in his lap, wrapped in his heavy coat. She felt so small and fragile. "We don't have to be apart for all those years. She could get well and we could grow up together then come to you when we're both grown." The sodden linen shirt stuck to his arms, freezing cold, and the hot tears stung his cheeks. "I could change things for the better."

"No," the elf put a gentle hand on his shoulder, "you can't. You know how the juice changes people. She's not a part of this world any more, she's like you or me and you need to let my friends look after her now. You know for a fact that you will be with her again. As soon as you get home to your own time you'll find her there waiting for you. Anyway," she explained, smiling gently, "The book changes because the future is not fixed but the past is. Once something has happened, nobody can change it."

"But it hasn't happened yet, has it?" Nicholai insisted, "This is all happening right now! The things that I remember are still in the future. If the future can be changed then surely I should be able to right now!"

"I think you already know the answer to that." The elf sat down beside the sobbing man, the snow clinging to her black hair, "I don't know how you got here but I do think I understand why. You can't change what happened in your own personal past because this is always what happened. Remember when you were a young boy? You remember meeting the strange, white-bearded old man, don't you?" Nicholai nodded, "That's because you were always here. You're not changing what happened by being here right now, you're just experiencing the same period of time from a different perspective. You're here now because you were always here."

"Then why can't I save her?" he pleaded, "Why can't I keep her safe like she always believed I could?"

"What are you doing right now?" asked the elf, gently, "See? You have her cradled in your arms and wrapped up warm. If you had not been here she would have died in the snow and nothing anyone could have done would have saved her. She was right to say that nothing bad could happen to her while you were around and that you would always be there to protect her. When her darkest time came, you were there! This is it!"

"You mean..." Nicholai struggled to understand what was

going on, "It was always me that saved her? All those years ago? I spent years thinking that I had failed her; let her down when she needed me most."

"And did that make you bitter?" his small but wise friend asked with a smile, "Did it make you into a bad, angry, lonely and selfish man? Some people, if they thought they'd lost something so precious would be angry at the whole world and take it out on anyone they met, becoming bitter and cold inside. Is that what happened to you? Or," she grinned, "did you become even more kind, gentle and loving than you were before? Doing good to others for her sake."

"You're right," Nicholai managed to smile, despite the circumstances, "of course you are. I was the one who found her and kept her safe until the elves could come and rescue her. This must have been what always happened."

"I know this isn't easy," the elf smiled, placing one of her hands on Nicholai's shoulder and stroking Annalina's soft hair with her other, "but it's what must happen. Here," she took a small bottle out of her bag, "give her some of this." Nicholai took the bottle; he did not have to be told what it was. It was a very diluted dose of the juice squeezed from the fruits of the tree from which his sleigh was made, the juice that he and Annalina had drank at their wedding to render them truly immortal. He understood that, many centuries before he was born, longer ago than was even possible to remember, the elves had eaten the fruit itself and had ceased to grow or age from that moment. As he took the bottle from the elf, he noticed something else in the small leather bag over her shoulder. It looked a little like a peach but smaller, with dark purple skin.

"What's that?" he asked, shifting Annalina's sleeping form in his arms so that he could use both hands to open the stoppered bottle.

"The last of its kind," the elf grinned, "we've been keeping it for when it was needed."

"I've never seen it before," he furrowed his brow, "I was told there was only the juice left, that's what Annalina was told too."

"There probably was by the time she was told about it!" she giggled, "now hurry up and give her the drink."

"How?" Nicholai asked, cradling his little sweetheart, the girl he had lost so many years ago only to find once more after almost an entire mortal lifetime had passed. "She's completely unconscious, barely breathing, I don't want her to choke."

"She won't, I promise." the elf smiled reassuringly. "The little of the juice that is mixed with that water would not be enough to restore a dead person to life but it is certainly enough to preserve the small spark of life that remains and restore her to health and...and to change her."

"Change her?" Nicholai asked, gently stroking Annalina's cheek as he tilted her head backwards and opened her mouth, ready to pour the life-giving liquid down her throat. "Change her how?"

"She will not be fully like us until the time is right, you know that," the elf smiled, "but to live among us she must become more like us than like her parents, to become a part of our world rather than theirs. That is why she could never go back."

"It seems so unfair."

"Her mortal life is over. If we were not here then she would die out here in the snow and there would be no future for the two of you. Not only would you live the rest of your life without your love but all the children of the world for all time would miss out on the joy that the two of you bring them together. You are a good and kind man, Nicholai, I can see that, but without her you could not hope to become what you have become. If we leave her here right now and walk away, she will die and you will be gone because you too would have died many centuries ago, alone in the cold. Is that what you want for either of you?"

The elf's words carried a sting but it was softened by the warmth in her voice. Nicholai understood that she was not trying to upset or threaten him, simply to explain why he must allow things to progress the way they were about it.

"I understand." he nodded quietly, "How much of this should I give her?"

"Half." the elf explained, "Those of us who are assigned to watch carry enough for both of you, as we never quite knew what was to happen or when, just that we must watch over you until the time was right."

Carefully, still cautious of pouring the liquid down her unconscious throat too quickly, Nicholai tilted the bottle and allowed a little over half the liquid, one large, viscous drop at a time, to fall into Annalina's open mouth. Although in such a deep sleep that she barely seemed to be breathing, Nicholai felt her swallow the drops and a slight smile tweaked the edges of her slightly-open mouth.

"What happens now?" Nicholai asked, worried that no change seemed to have taken place in her appearance or condition and worrying that he had somehow got things wrong and unwittingly frustrated the path of destiny.

"Just wait," the elf smiled, "and watch." Having never witnessed such an event for herself either, the elf leant forward to watch with interest. For a few minutes which, for Nicholai, stretched on for an age, nothing at all seemed to happen but then, almost imperceptibly at first but becoming increasingly obvious with every passing second, Annalina's face began to glow red as if she were being burned up by fever. She began to shiver and to sweat. Nicholai clutched her tightly to his chest and cradled her as the shaking subsided and her face returned to a more normal colour, albeit far healthier and rosier than it had ever been before.

"It's done." the elf grinned, "She is one of us now, part of our world. We need to take her to the caves."

"They're a long way from here." Nicholai frowned, "and I do not think the sleigh is in any fit state to fly. What are we to do?"

"It's many day's walk," the elf admitted, "it took me the better part of a summer to reach here when it was my turn to watch over you." Nicholai felt a little embarrassed at this, having personally taken over thirty years to reach the caves but then, he thought to himself, he had not known where he was headed. Perhaps, even if he had found the caves within weeks, he would not have been allowed to see the entrance or find his way inside as he had not yet learned the lessons he was destined to learn on his travels. One thing he had learned from his time amongst the elves was that, however random and coincidental events may appear at the time, they were always part of a greater plan, the path of his life along which he was destined to travel.

"I think," the elf exclaimed, her eyes lighting up with excitement, "that I understand now why that last piece of fruit is in the bag!" Taking it out and holding it aloft triumphantly, she called to Sleipnir who happily accepted the tasty treat from her hand.

Thirteen

"Are you sure this is going to work?" Nicholai asked, climbing onto Sleipnir's back having helped the elf up and laid Annalina gently across the beast's shoulders where the elf could hold onto her trough their journey.

"It's the reason your reindeer can fly, isn't it?" the elf grinned, "Why shouldn't it work for a horse too?"

"What about afterwards?" Nicholai asked, "Won't an immortal, flying horse raise a few eyebrows when I take him back?"

"So don't take him back!" suggested the elf, "You know that you never saw him again after this night and, with everything else that's going on, I doubt his disappearance will be particularly high on anyone's priorities! If anyone even notices he's gone, they'll probably just think he got spooked by the storm and ran away."

"You think I could?" Nicholai asked, feeling just for a moment like a little boy again at the thought of being able to keep his childhood friend forever, "Could I bring him back with me to my time?"

"Perhaps," the elf mused, "or if you can't then he can wait for you. He won't get any older, any more than the reindeer do, or you or me for that matter. But for now, we need to concentrate on getting back to the caves where she can be looked after. You know the way?"

"Like the back of my hand!" Nicholai grinned, feeling more relaxed with every passing second now that he could see that the situation was in hand and that Annalina was going to be safe. "But I've never ridden a flying horse before."

"Neither have I!" giggled the elf, "but I'm sure it can't be that different from riding a normal one, just a little higher up!"

"I guess so." Nicholai grinned, "I don't normally fly in normal time and I normally make a lot of stops along the way but I think, if I've worked it out correctly, it should take about an hour to fly there from here. You'd better hold tight." he cautioned, "Here we go!"

As his master gave a nudge with his heel to let him know he was ready to go, Sleipnir, who was feeling stronger and more energetic than ever before, began to gallop forward despite the snow which continued to fall heavily all around them. As the two riders leant forwards and Nicholai gave a flick of the reins, the horse's hooves began to rise above the ground and soon they were flying through the air, high above the trees and soon above even the dark clouds from which the snow was falling. Although a little different from flying in a sleigh, Nicholai did not find it too difficult to ride and steer the flying horse who, far from being frightened by being so high up, seemed to greatly be enjoying the new-found freedom of being able to gallop through the air. Soon enough, despite not being able to see much of the ground beneath them, Nicholai's navigational skills told him that they were almost above the pine forest surrounding the entrance to the caves he called home.

Suddenly, it occurred to him that, although the caves themselves would not have moved, nobody in them would know him and they may look very different inside. Would, he wondered, there even be space for him to land? In all the time he had known of the place, there had been a clearing outside the large doors through which the sleigh would be pulled for his annual flight but, as his elf companion had told him, the sleigh was many years away from being finished and, if the clearing was not natural, they may not have prepared it yet. Luckily, he thought to himself, a horse would require a far smaller space in which to land than the sleigh with its team of eight reindeer.

As they descended through the clouds, Nicholai was relieved to see that the clearing looked just as it did in his own time. The trees around were a little different, as was to be expected, but the grassy space before the large wooden doors looked the same as ever. As he guided Sleipnir down, Nicholai wondered what was to be done with the sleigh that he had left back in the forest. It seemed that, when the lightning had struck his sleigh, it had only sent the sleigh itself and those actually inside it back, leaving the reindeer behind in their own time. He hoped that their natural instincts would prompt them to return home but he would have to worry about them later.

Surprisingly gently, considering that he had never flown, let alone landed before, Sleipnir's hooves made contact with the ground and he trotted in a small circle before coming to a complete stop. Nicholai quickly jumped down from his mount and scooped Annalina up in his arms. The elf scrambled down and ran to catch up with him as he strode towards the enormous wooden doors through which the sleigh normally emerged. There was a smaller door set into them through which the elves could come and go, in his time remodelled to be large enough for him and his wife but currently still only big enough for a child or an elf to pass through comfortably, and he expected to have to send his elf companion in first to gather the others but, as they approached, the doors began to slowly open inwards, bathing the clearing in the warm, orange light from within the caves.

From inside, a small group of elves emerged, peering curiously at their visitor with his flying steed and the small bundle in his arms, knowing all too well what that bundle was. Looking at their faces, Nicholai felt strangely uncomfortable, as if he were intruding into another's life. All the faces looking up at him were the faces of his friends, people he had known and lived with for more than three centuries, yet none of them knew him, not yet anyway.

There was something else different about the elves too, not just the lack of recognition on their faces that struck Nicholai as unfamiliar. In his time, all the elves wore dresses like those favoured by his wife. She had told him that she had started passing the many lovely dresses they made for her onto them when she grew out of them but, as she got older and her dresses started to be far too large for even the tallest of the elves, they had started making them for themselves. Those who now came out to meet him, however, were all dressed in identical, plain brown tunics, the only colour coming from their bright red hats, a fashion which had survived into his own time alongside their new dresses, and the necklaces and bracelets woven from colourful threads that many of them wore.

One thing that had always struck him about the elves was their ability to adapt to new events and changing circumstances. While none of them yet knew him and it was highly unlikely that they had been expecting him to turn up under these circumstances, they seemed perfectly accepting of the situation and greeted him like an honoured guest.

None of them seemed to need to be told what was happening. Instead, they parted to let the trio through the doors. As the elf who had accompanied Nicholai on the journey led the way to the cave which was to become Annalina's bedroom, they all scurried away to prepare everything they would need to care for her and the things that she would need when she woke up.

As he had noticed with the elves themselves, Nicholai was struck by how little colour there was in the caves. The young boy who he knew would now be waking up to the cruel revelation that the nightmare of the night before had been real and resolving not to rest until he had found his lost love, even if it meant walking the earth for the rest of eternity, had never seen the caves like this. Nicholai's first view of the place he now called home had come some twenty years later, by which time Annalina's influence had spread throughout the community, with all the carvings brightly painted and the elves all dressed in colourful dresses like her own.

One thing that had not changed over time, he was relieved to see, was the actual layout of the caves themselves. He easily found his way to the room he knew as his bedroom, glancing into other rooms as he walked briskly down the corridor, intrigued at how different they looked from his time. He knew the room would be plainer than he knew it, and lacking the doorway he had helped to cut through the rock into the large chamber beyond that was now his library and study, but he was not quite prepared for just how sparse it was.

All that he could see in the room was a bed. The same bed he and Annalina still slept in but looking very different. Like all the other carvings around the caves, it was unpainted. With the exception of the hats and woven bands that the elves wore, there seemed to be no colour in the caves at all. The decoration in the caves from his own time must, he realised, have been down to Annalina's influence. Beside the bed was a small table but there was nothing else in the room. Gone were the enormous, carved wardrobes where Annalina kept her vast array of dresses and in which he kept his own far more modest collection of clothes, gone was the dressing table and the large bookcases which stretched almost to the roof of the cave.

Although plain, the bed still looked soft and comfortable. Feeling Annalina's fragile heartbeat becoming stronger with every passing moment, Nicholai gently laid his future bride down on the bed and pulled a blanket over her like a loving parent before leaning down and kissing her gently on the forehead and whispering to her.

"Rest well, my sweet forest rose."

Fourteen

"What will you do now?" the elf who had accompanied him up through the last few days asked, taking his hand and squeezing it comfortingly. As he had often done in the past, Nicholai reflected on how, despite the fact that the elves all looked like young children and retained their innocent sense of wonder and excitement, their great age still shone through and there were times when they could feel, to Nicholai, like surrogate parents or even grandparents. This was one of those moments.

"I don't know." he admitted quietly. "I need time to think." Since waking up to find himself stranded in his own past, events had unfolded so fast that Nicholai had had no choice but to simply react to what was happening around him. There had been no time to make plans or come up with any kind of strategy about how to put things right.

"You can't think on an empty stomach!" the elf grinned. "Come on, we'll get you some food and drink then you can decide what you're going to do next."

"Are you sure that will be all right?" Nicholai asked, concerned, "I can't be here when she wakes up, it would confuse everything."

"Do you always worry this much?" giggled his friend, "Surely you understand that nobody can change the past? Things are as they are and always have been. You rescued her and brought her here today because you always did. Don't you remember meeting yourself as a small boy?"

"I do." Nicholai admitted, "I just didn't realise it until now."

"In your time, the two of you are together, right?"

"Yes. I eventually found my way here and we've been together ever since."

"And," the elf asked, patiently, "in that time, did she ever mention meeting a strange old man shortly after she first arrived here?"

"No," confirmed Nicholai, "and I don't suppose that's the sort of thing she would have forgotten."

"Then I think it's fairly safe to assume that you won't be here by the time she wakes up and that you have time to come and share a meal with us!" Nicholai smiled warmly, with a sense of relief. The elves always had such a sensible, matter-of-fact way of looking at things. In all the time he had lived with them, he had never known them to seem overwhelmed by any situation. They simply took what life threw at them as it came and adapted to suit the circumstances. "Anyway," the elf continued, "she's recovering from a very traumatic experience. She really was very close to death. Her body will need to repair itself now and for that she will need plenty of rest. I don't think she'll be waking up for two or three days yet but don't worry," she squeezed his hand again, "we'll watch over her and make sure she recovers well. I promise we won't let anything bad happen to her."

"I know you won't." Nicholai smiled. "I understand that now. I know nothing bad will happen to her now because we have that wonderful future together and it's a future I'm determined to get back to but, for now," he grinned, "I think I will take you up on that invitation of breakfast!"

"Why don't you go and have a swim while we get everything ready?" his friend suggested, "I'm sure you know where the lagoon is? There's some warm, dry blankets there you can use and we'll get some new clothes for you made while you're gone. Then, when you're refreshed and clean, we can eat!"

Having lived for so long with the elves, Nicholai knew that they were incredibly fast when it came to making clothes. Annalina had told him how, when she first arrived, they had created a whole wardrobe full of clothes for her in the course of one night so he understood that having a new shirt and trousers ready for him in half an hour or so would be no challenge to them what so ever.

Gratefully, Nicholai made his way down the corridor towards the wonderful, underground lake with its warm springs bubbling waterfalls. Alone in the vast cave, he peeled off the clothes had had become practically stuck to him over the course of his horseback ride through the snow then slipped into the water and allowed it to soothe his aching muscles. Doing something so ordinary, something he did practically every day of his life, made him feel safe somehow. This cavern seemed to be the one part of the network of caves that had not changed at all from this time to his own and, for a few minutes as he swam gently around, the sound of his own splashes echoing off the vaulted roof of the cave, Nicholai was able to put the strangeness and drama of the last few days from his mind. Closing his eyes and floating, almost asleep but conscious enough to stay afloat, Nicholai was only vaguely aware of the small group of elves who came in to take away his soiled clothes. This was the first time since the storm that he had really had an opportunity to take stock of what had happened to him.

When flying his sleigh, Nicholai moved outside of normal time, imperceptible to mortals, the fact that he had been travelling at all only evidenced by the gifts he left behind. The storm, however, had seemed to occupy the same parallel time-stream to his own and was therefore not simply a natural weather event. His sleigh was carved from the fallen wood of the very same tree which had provided the fruit which had granted immortality, over many centuries, to the terrifying Krampus, the Pieten, the elves and, of course, to himself and his beloved Annalina. Neither he nor the elves had ever been able to find any explanation for why the tree had possessed those unique qualities and how it had come to be in the first place. But now Nicholai was beginning to suspect that the storm, or one like it, had somehow caused it to come into being. If he could discover what caused the storm, or where it had come from, then, Nicholai hoped, it may hold the key to getting him back home.

The troubling thoughts, however, were eclipsed by the enormous feeling of relief that was washing over him, like the soothing water. Since that terrible night which he had just been forced to re-live, he had carried with him a huge weight of guilt. Annalina, for as long as she had been able to speak, had constantly assured him that she knew nothing bad could ever happen to her when he was around as she knew he would always protect her yet, on that night, or so he believed, he had failed her. She had been lost in the snow and most likely died because he had not been able to save her. Even years later when they were reunited and he learned that she had been kept safe by the elves, he still felt a cold lump in his stomach, believing that her survival had been in spite of his inadequacy as a protector. Now that lump and the weight on his shoulders was gone. It may not have been how either of them expected, but he had been there to save her that night and she had survived because of his actions.

With this new lightness in his soul, Nicholai enjoyed the warm, cleansing feel of the water which seemed to be washing away not only the dirt and grime he had accumulated over the last day or so but also all the stress, fear and confusion. So relaxed was he that he felt as if he could stay floating in that wonderful underground lake forever. All too soon, however, his stomach began to remind him of just how long it had been since he'd eaten so he heaved himself out of the water, wrapped a warm blanket around his waist and another around his shoulders to catch the drips from his thick, long hair which was already starting to dry in the warmth of the subterranean air. A little way down the corridor, he noticed that a wooden peg had been driven into the wall and, hanging from it was a brand new suit of clothes made especially for him while he had been bathing.

Chuckling, Nicholai took the clothes down from the hook and marvelled again at how creative the elves were and the amount of effort they put into any project, whether it was needed or not. While a simple pair of trousers and a shirt would have sufficed, they had made him a long waistcoat in red, decorated with elaborate gold stitching and a pair of trousers to match. The shirt, made from thin white cotton to make it comfortable in the warmth of the caves, was also decorated around the collar and cuffs with the gold embroidery. In the pocket of the trousers, Nicholai found a metal comb which he used to neaten his now-dry hair and beard before making his way down the strange yet familiar corridors to the main chamber where he was sure a delicious breakfast would be waiting for him.

"Are you all right?" the small elf asked, taking Nicholai's hand again as she found him in the doorway of what would one day be his bedroom, watching Annalina gently sleeping in the large bed as she recovered from the deadly trauma she had suffered only hours before. The elf could see that her friend's eyes were glazed with tears; the same tears which streaked his cheeks dampened the beard on his cheeks.

"I'm sorry." he managed to smile as he looked down at her, "I know everything will work out. I just can't help remembering what this time felt like the first time around, when I lost her. She and I are about to spend so many years apart. It really doesn't seem fair."

"From what you've told me," the elf smiled reassuringly, "the time apart only made your love for each other grow stronger. You never forgot each other and neither of you ever lost hope that you would one day be together again."

"I know." He smiled again, "It's just that, well," he sighed, "since I came here the first time, from my point of view at least, we've not spent more than one night apart and now I don't know how long it's going to be before I see her again."

"But you know that you will." the elf smiled again, squeezing his hand encouragingly like his father used to when he was little and was beginning to get tired on a long walk. "Surely your life so far has proved that the love between you is too strong for you to be kept apart forever. Whatever and however long it takes, I know, and I'm sure you do too, that you will be together again.

"You're right." Nicholai took one last look at the sleeping girl before turning and allowing the elf to lead him down a corridor to the chamber where the sleigh was normally housed and where now, he realised, the very same sleigh would be under construction.

Sixteen

"Well," Nicholai knelt down to hug his friend and smiled warmly at the whole group of tunic-clad elves who had come to see him off, "I suppose this is goodbye, for now at least. I expect it will be strange for you, won't it, when you see me again? You'll know me but I won't know you."

"When you've been around as long as we have," his friend giggled, "you begin to think of time as little differently. You know about the book, don't you?"

"Of course I do!" Nicholai grinned, "Very useful thing, that book! But I thought Annalina was the only one who could read it properly?"

"She is," shrugged the elf, "or she will be anyway, but we can still use it to see pictures of the future. The possible future, anyway. Makes it easier to think of time as a story that can be dipped in and out of. After all," she chuckled, "you're here in your own past right now, but it's a past that your future self, as you are now, was always a part of! If that doesn't prove that time isn't just a straight line, then I don't know what does."

"Very true!" Nicholai chuckled, standing up, "You have a very good point there."

"Anyway," the dark-haired elf grinned, "I'm coming with you!"

"What do you mean?" Nicholai asked, "You can't come into the future with me, I know you back in my own time. If you travel with me then you won't be there." He shook his head, slightly bewildered by the thought he had just tried to give voice to.

"Of course I'm not coming to the future!" she shook her own head, amused at how foolish and easily confused her new friend could be at times, although she supposed that it was acceptable for him to be confused under the circumstances. "But I'm coming with you to make sure the sleigh is hidden safely and to see that you get safely back to your own time. We can't have you just flying around on your own, chasing every storm for years, can we? Who knows what kind of trouble you might get into!"

"Very well then." Nicholai grinned, "I can't say I wouldn't be glad of the company. What about the rest of you?" he turned to the rest of the elves who had gathered to see him off, "Are you all coming?"

"We could," one of them teased, "but that would probably make it quite hard for you to travel around unnoticed. Besides," she grinned as the others giggled, "there's lots of work to be done here and we have a guest to look after!"

With the temporary goodbyes said, one of the taller elves, with long, light-brown hair in a plait down her back, pulled the lever which caused the heavy, oak doors to slowly swing open. Outside in the clearing, Sleipnir was waiting, munching contentedly on a pile of hay, a fine new saddle made from dark green leather with polished brass accents. There seemed really to be no limits to the elves' creativity. As the doors opened, he looked up and saw his master. Patting his childhood friend on the neck, Nicholai noticed that the saddle had been made for two, with seats for one adult and a child-sized person in front.

"I see you had this planned?" Nicholai chuckled. The elf said nothing but grinned as he lifted her onto the saddle then climbed up behind her.

Pausing to wave at the assembled elves, Nicholai tugged the green leather reins and Sleipnir began to run towards the far side of the clearing, taking off half way across and rising into the air above the trees, the leaves on the uppermost branches rustling in the wind that gushed beneath him as he soared.

With his equine friend apparently as relaxed with the idea of flying as he had been before, Nicholai took the opportunity to enjoy the spectacular views over the forests. It had been a matter of hours since he had flown this same route in the opposite direction but then he had been desperately trying to get Annalina to safety, focussed only on reaching the caves and not able to enjoy or even notice the view. Now, things were different. Annalina was safely sleeping, watched over by the elves and was about to start an exciting new life while he was on his way to tie up a few loose ends before seeking out the freak storm that would be able to send him home and back into the arms of his beloved wife.

Seventeen

Taking care that there was nobody around to witness them landing, Nicholai guided Sleipnir down at the edge of the woodland in which he knew that the sleigh was still hidden under a heap of earth.

"I must admit," Nicholai explained sheepishly, "I haven't really thought about what we're going to do now. We could just make sure it's still there and leave it buried, then I can dig it up when I get home but there's no guarantee it wouldn't be found in the meantime."

"Well, was it?"

"What do you mean?" Nicholai was puzzled.

"Well," the elf grinned teasingly, "surely if a beautifully carved wooden sleigh that seemed to be able to fly was found, it would be pretty big news, wouldn't it?" Nicholai nodded his head in agreement, "And, if everything works out as I expect it will," continued his friend, "then you and what you do will be very well-known by the time you come from."

"Also true." Nicholai agreed, nodding.

"So, don't you think if a sleigh like this were to be found, people might at least speculate that it was yours?"

"Most likely." chuckled Nicholai, "It's probably the most famous sleigh in the world, despite the fact that nobody has ever seen it!"

"Things like this have a way of getting out don't they?" the elf teased. "Anyway, my point is that, if your sleigh were to be discovered any time between now and the storm, people around the world would have been talking about it."

"I suppose they would."

"And if everybody was talking about it, then don't you think you would have heard about it?"

"It would have got back to me sooner or later." conceded Nicholai. As the world had moved on around them, he and Annalina had made an effort to remain aware of what was going on in the world. If nothing else, it was important to know about the latest trends so that they would know what kind of toys the children would be wanting. There was no doubt that if Santa Claus' sleigh, or something closely resembling, it were to be found, then the news would indeed be reported around the world and there was no way that he would not have heard about it. "So what are you saying?"

"I'm saying, silly man," the elf sighed, but with a patient smile on her face, "that if the sleigh gets found from wherever you happen to hide it, then you would know. You understand, don't you, that everything that's happening now is what always happened, you just didn't know about it at the time?" Nicholai nodded. "Well the fact that you never heard about the sleigh being discovered means that, wherever you end up hiding it, it stays safely hidden until you go back for it!"

"I see!" Nicholai exclaimed, finally understanding, "But the question still remains, where should we hide it?"

"It needs to be somewhere safe and secure," the elf mused, "but somewhere that will be easy for you to find again. Forests, buildings and even the landscape in general change over time. Once you're back in your own time, you're going to need to be able to find it."

"I do have one idea." pondered Nicholai, stroking his beard in the way he always did when deep in thought, "There are some caves not far from here, my father always warned me they were dangerous and not to play near them. I think they may have once been part of a mine or something like that, a long time before I was born. I've always kept an eye on this area over the years and I know that it doesn't get changed that much. Oh, the forest gets smaller, more houses are built and there are some big roads nearby in my time, but fundamentally it remains the same."

"You think if we put the sleigh in a cave then it will be safe there for however long it needs to stay?"

"Well, as you said," Nicholai grinned, "I at least know it won't be discovered! I can't actually think of anywhere safer for it. If the entrance to the caves is sealed up by the time I get there, then I'm sure we'll be able to crack our way into it. After all," he chuckled, "there are several more rooms in our home in my time than there are right now. Hollowing out caves is something of a speciality of ours, in my time at least!"

"Then I'd say it's a splendid idea!"

"There's just one problem." Nicholai frowned. "How are we supposed to get the sleigh there? I can't make it fly without Annalina and it's far too heavy for the two of us to move."

"We have Sleipnir!" his friend reminded him, "Or had you forgotten about him?"

"He's a strong beast all right," Nicholai reflected, "but not as strong as eight reindeer! And, as far as I know, they weren't transported when the sleigh was. Only those of us inside the sleigh came back in time."

"The fruit will have made him stronger than he was before," explained the elf, "and we're not going to ask him to pull the sleigh through the air, just along the ground. But wait a minute!" she exclaimed as Nicholai's words sunk in, "What do you mean 'Those of us who were in the sleigh'? It wasn't just you? Was one of us in the sleigh too?"

"Not you, no." Nicholai admitted, realising that he was going to have to tell his friend about the Pieten and hope that she would not react too badly to them. Annalina had told him that, when she first met them, the elves had a deep mistrust of the Pieten and had warned her to stay away from them. After she had got to know them for herself and spent some time with them, she had realised that they and the elves were not so different after all and, it had turned out, what the elves saw as their destructive tendencies was actually a very positive curiosity about how things work and are put together.

In Nicholai's time, the two communities were very close and the Pieten's curiosity had been channelled into creativity. Nicholai understood, however, that the elf who now accompanied him did not yet have these experiences and may still be afraid of his two, small, hairy friends. He hoped that he would be able to show her that they were friendly, even if she assumed they were unusual and unique amongst their race.

"You might as well come out now!" Nicholai called up into the trees.

"Who are you talking to?" asked the elf, her eyes wide with curiosity.

"My friends!" Nicholai grinned; pleased that, for once, he was the one who knew and understood what was going on. "I always know when they're nearby. They're pretty good at hiding from most people, but I always know."

To the elf's surprise, the two little fellows jumped down from the branches of the trees above them. Nicholai had supposed that Sleipnir might have been startled by these unusual new arrivals, but he seemed to accept them with the same placid nonchalance as he had accepted all the peculiar new developments of the last few days. Discovering that his master was now a fully grown man and being given the ability to fly did not seem to have struck Sleipnir as being particularly remarkable. Having taken all these in his stride, therefore, the arrival of the little men was far from shocking.

"Aren't those...?" the elf asked, nervously. "What were they doing with you?"

"They're my friends!" Nicholai explained with a grin, "Don't worry, I know you don't have much to do with them, not yet anyway. But trust me on this. They're my friends and they're here to help us."

Kneeling down, Nicholai spoke quickly to the small men in their own language. While they could understand Annalina and Nicholai's native tongue quite well, only a few of them could speak it, and then only with a very limited vocabulary. Out of courtesy, Nicholai had learned their language and encouraged the others to do likewise. The ability to pick up new languages was a talent he had acquired on his travels so, despite the strangeness of the Pieten tongue; he had become reasonably fluent in it quite easily. Annalina had found it a little harder but had worked until she was almost as proficient as he was. The elves, who had lived for centuries speaking only their own language, which luckily was very similar to Annalina and Nicholai's, had found it almost impossible to learn the Pieten language beyond a very basic level, but the Pieten appreciated their effort and took it as a mark of respect.

"I was asking them to dig out the sleigh as best they can." Nicholai explained as he stood up and the Pieten scampered off into the woods. "They have sharp, very hard claws so they're extremely good at digging."

"You came back then?" The friendly voice caught both Nicholai and his small friend by surprise and they turned in unison to see who had spoken.

Eighteen

"Don't worry." The strong-looking man assured the shocked pair, "I'm here to help you. Not quite sure what I can do as I'm not entirely sure what it is you're doing here but, if there's any way I can help, then I will."

"Joseph?" Nicholai asked, recognising the man who had been like a second father to him during his childhood. As a boy, he had thought Joseph was quite old but now, looking at him through his older eyes, he realised that he was actually no older than his own apparent age. Realising he had just called out the name of a man he had not officially been introduced to, Nicholai tried to cover. "Didn't I see you at the house earlier? I'm sure the children were talking about you."

"Don't worry." Joseph smiled, "I know who you are. It took me a little while to work it out but when I saw how much Sleipnir seems to like you, something clicked in my brain and I realised. I've spent enough time with you to recognise you however old you get. I have no idea how you got here but I'm guessing it wasn't on purpose and, if there's anything I can do to help you then, as always, I'm happy to."

"Wait a minute!" Nicholai was shocked, "You know me? Why did you recognise me when my parents didn't?"

"They probably would have done if you'd been with them for longer." Joseph shrugged. "I think your mother was starting to. If she were to see you again now that, well, you have gone, she might realise."

"That wouldn't be good for any of us." Nicholai reminded him, sadly. "It's not good for people to know too much about their own futures."

"I understand that." Joseph nodded, "I promise that I will keep your secret. Like I said, I don't know how you got here but I'm happy to help. Who's your young friend here?" He turned and smiled at the elf, "Don't you work in the stables?"

"I did for a while." she admitted with a giggle, "But I'm not exactly young. I'm...well I suppose you would call me an elf. I was here watching this young man and his little sweetheart." She hugged Nicholai's arm, "As you can probably tell, they both turn out to be quite important and we needed to make sure that nothing would happen to them."

"You seem to be taking this all quite calmly." Nicholai observed, intrigued as to why his old friend would accept these remarkable revelations as if they were an every-day occurrence.

"I've been around for a while," Joseph winked, "and seen some strange and remarkable things in my time. Oh, not like you two!" he chuckled, "I'm quite normal in that sense, mortal as they come. But," he grinned, "Let's just say it takes a lot to surprise me!"

"You never mentioned anything unusual when I was a boy?" Nicholai challenged, intrigued to discover this previously unknown side to his oldest friend.

"Would you have believed me if I had?"

"Well, since you put it like that..." Nicholai replied with a chuckle.

"Plus," Joseph continued, in a darker tone, "Not everything magical is as good and joyful as you two and your friends. There are some things your parents would not have thanked me for telling you about."

"What happened to you?" the elf asked, reaching up to touch the kind man's face and seeing the long-buried fear in his eyes, "What did you see?"

"That's a story for another time." Joseph replied quietly, "One I pray that you'll never have to hear."

"Thank you." Nicholai clasped his friend's shoulders, "For caring for me when I was a boy and for helping me again now. Whatever it was that happened to you in the past, I hope that you have been able to make your peace with it."

"It's very rare that no good results from a situation." Joseph smiled his usual, jovial self once more. "After all, if I hadn't...well, if that hadn't happened then I might have had a much harder time recognising and accepting you and your friend here!"

"And again I thank you." Nicholai smiled warmly.

"So Annalina is...?" Joseph asked, remembering the horror and despair of the night before when the little girl he loved as a daughter had gone missing.

"She's safe," the elf assured him, "and she's got a great future ahead of her. I don't think she'll ever be able to come back here," she explained, a little sadly, "but you can be sure that she will have a wonderful, long future and will never forget the kindness you have shown her."

"That's good enough for me." Joseph smiled, wishing he could run to Annalina's parents' farm and tell them that their daughter was safe but knowing that he must not, hoping that he would be able to support and reassure them in other ways. "Now, is anybody going to tell me what you're doing here right now?"

Nineteen

"That's a magnificent vehicle all right!" Joseph exclaimed, seeing the sleigh for the first time. The sight of the tired but happy Pieten who had spent the last hour or so digging it out and polishing up the scorched woodwork with the wiry fur on their arms did not seem to faze Joseph at all. Nicholai couldn't help but wonder exactly what it was that Joseph had encountered in his past that had left his mind so open to ideas that would have caused most normal mortals to collapse in shock but his old friend had made it clear enough that he did not wish to discuss it or be reminded of that incident, whatever it had been. "I've explored the old mine a little bit in the past," Joseph continued, "and I'm certain there are some big enough chambers to store it in, places where the miners used to keep their tools or where they'd store what they dug up before taking it to the surface. Once it's down there, we can move some of the bigger rocks to cover the entrance so that, even if anyone goes poking about down there, they won't be able to get to it. It should be nice and dry down there," he continued, his years of maintaining Nicholai's family's property having taught him to think in practical terms about such matters, "but I'm a little worried about the damage to the varnish. Here, you see?" he ran his fingers along the edge of the scorched area and the resinous finish crumbled beneath his fingers. "I'm worried the wood might start rotting."

"I wouldn't worry too much about that." Nicholai smiled, "It's not exactly made from normal wood. I've been using it for several lifetimes now and it never seems to age at all. It's as if the wood is still alive and can repair itself. I suspect, by the time I get back to it, it will be good as new. I'm not even sure that's actually varnish on the outside anyway." With his finger nail, he scraped away some of the charred wood, revealing the undamaged layer beneath which immediately began weeping a kind of viscous sap. "It's started already." Nicholai pointed out. "I really don't think that's going to be a problem."

"Good." Joseph nodded in a business-like fashion. "Although I notice that it didn't seem to start healing until you scraped away the damage. Here's an idea." he suggested, brightly, happy that he had found a way to play a bigger role in the exciting story that his young friend's future clearly was to be, "We'll take it down there now but we won't seal it in, just throw some dark blankets over it or something to keep it hidden. When things are quiet on the estate, I'll go down there and do as much as I can to get it cleaned up, scrape off the burned stuff and suchlike. When I feel like I've done as much as I can, then I'll seal it up for you to find."

"You would do that for me?" Nicholai asked, genuinely moved at the amount of effort his old friend was prepared to go to on his behalf.

"Of course I would, young master." Joseph smiled, "It would be an honour to be a part of your mission." Both men beamed at each other and it made the elf feel warm inside to see the obvious affection between the two. The bond they had shared when Nicholai was a child was clearly still there, despite the fact that Nicholai had not seen him in several mortal lifetimes and, from Joseph's perspective, Nicholai had gone from a young boy on the cusp of manhood to middle-aged in a heartbeat. Neither fact seemed to have in any way diminished the bond of surrogate father and son that existed between them.

"There's only one problem that I can see." Joseph stroked his chin which made the elf giggle as she realised that it was clearly from Joseph that Nicholai had adopted the mannerism.

"Oh?" Nicholai furrowed his brow.

"Well, getting the sleigh down into the caves isn't going to be too much of an issue." Joseph explained, "The entrance is wide enough and some of the chambers down there are as big as a stable but how are we going to get it to the cave entrance?"

"We've got Sleipnir." Nicholai pointed out, remembering what the elf had told him not long before, "He should be easily strong enough to pull it. He's far stronger now than he was yesterday and it's not really that far we need to move it, if my memory serves correctly."

"You're missing the point." Joseph continued, patiently, "Look around you! I can tell from the broken branches and the way it's sitting in this crater," he nodded towards the bowl-shaped dip in the ground that the Pieten had cleared around the sleigh to free it from its muddy prison, "that it got here by dropping out the sky. Don't ask me how you got it up there in the first place but if I can accept that you're young Master Nicholai from the future, she's an elf," he inclined his head towards Nicholai's friend, "and, well, as for you two," he grinned at the Pieten, "I'm not quite sure what you are but any friend of Nicholai's is a friend of mine. Anyway," he continued, "my point is that if I can accept all these things, adding a flying sleigh to the list isn't too much of a stretch. But," he turned to Nicholai, his voice taking on a slightly more serious tone, "assuming that, if you could fly this thing out of here then you would have done so already, how are we going to get it out of the woods?"

Hearing this question, the two Pieten began to jump around excitedly, waving their hands to get Nicholai's attention and chattering loudly to indicate they had a suggestion. Turning to them, Nicholai listened carefully as they explained their plan. Joseph couldn't help being amused at the wildly animated mannerisms of the little men. Whatever their suggestion might be, they certainly seemed proud of it.

"They ask what kind of rock is beneath us." Nicholai explained to Joseph who, he was well aware, could not understand any of the Pieten's strange language. Joseph pondered for a moment.

"Sandstone, I think." he replied, "Like the mine." Nicholai nodded thoughtfully. "My father dug a well nearby when I was a lad," Joseph continued, "and I remember big piles of sand around the top." Nicholai was pleased to hear this. If the rock beneath his original home was similar enough to that of the caves in which he lived then the Pieten's plan could just work.

Quickly, Nicholai explained to Joseph that the Pieten planned to dig down though the ground in front of the sleigh and dig a tunnel linking where they now stood to the caves where it had been agreed the sleigh would be hidden for safe-keeping. Once the tunnel was completed, Sleipnir would be able to pull the sleigh underground to where it would be kept until Nicholai retrieved it back in his own time.

"It would take a year or more to tunnel that far." Joseph objected, "The entrance to the caves is nearly a mile from here."

"They're faster than you think!" Nicholai grinned. "And anyway, I'm pretty sure the caves extend back in this direction. It shouldn't take them more than a day to break through."

"If you say so!" Joseph chuckled. "After all, I can only begin to imagine the things you have seen in your lifetime! Just how old are you now, anyway?"

"A lot older than I look!" Nicholai winked. "In all honesty, I gave up counting a while back but I stopped physically ageing when I was a just a little younger than you are now." He ran his fingers through his thick white hair and chuckled. "This went white before its time, really, but I suppose it lends me a certain air of wisdom!"

"And is travelling through time something you do a lot?" Joseph asked, accepting the fact of Nicholai's immortality apparently as easily as he had accepted the existence of elves and flying sleighs.

"Actually no." admitted Nicholai. "If anything, I usually travel outside of time! This is as strange for me as it is for you." Smiling, he turned to the Pieten and spoke quickly in their own language, confirming to them that the rock was indeed of a kind that would be easy enough for them to tunnel through with their hard, sharp claws.

"Do you think there's anything we can do to help?" the elf asked, wondering how they were supposed to fill the time while the

Pieten, whom she still regarded with some suspicion, carried out their task. Fortunately, the snow had not settled nearly as heavily in the forest as it had done out in the fields where there was no canopy of trees to obstruct it and the little that had settled in the area around the sleigh had, in the subsequent days, frozen to an icy powder which was easy enough to brush aside. Looking down, Nicholai noticed that already a significant pile of sand was starting to form above the hole that his diminutive friends had started to carve out, the soil and sand already covering the snow.

"Looks like it might be a good idea start moving some of this." Nicholai inclined his head downwards to indicate the mounting pile, "Otherwise, it won't be too long before the sleigh is buried again! Joseph," he turned to his friend, "do you have any buckets we could borrow?"

Twenty

The first orange rays of dawn sunlight were beginning to show above the trees when the Pieten finally emerged from the new tunnel, indicating excitedly to Nicholai that they had completed the task and made a passageway from the middle of the forest to the caves. As the little men had worked, the rest of the party had worked as hard as they could shifting the piles of loose sand away from the opening of the tunnel into neat heaps nearby, taking it in turns to go and check on Sleipnir who had been left tethered quite contentedly at the edge of the woods. When it was time to move the sleigh, he would have to be led carefully between all the trees but there seemed little point in doing so until they were ready for him.

Once the sleigh was in position, they knew that the tunnel would have to be filled in again but Joseph had promised them that he would see to that, maybe getting some of the hired hands from the estate to help out. He wasn't sure what he would tell them about where the tunnel had come from but was confident that he would be able to think of some plausible explanation.

"There!" Joseph smiled, pouring out the last bucket of sand onto the heap he had been building between two large trees. "Looks like we're about ready to go." Standing at the mouth of the tunnel which sloped down for some distance before gently levelling out, he peered down into it while the Pieten shook themselves and scratched at their wiry fur to dislodge all the stray grains. "It's dark down there." he observed, "We're going to need some lanterns. Give me half an hour," he smiled, "and I'll be back with some."

"Won't people wonder what you're doing with lanterns in the daylight?" the elf asked, hoping that this activity, strange to anyone who might be observing it, would not give them away.

"I wouldn't have thought so." Joseph smiled, a little sadly, "Most people are still too distracted by...well, by what happened in the storm. I doubt anyone will notice what I'm doing. Speaking of the storm," he turned to Nicholai, "I have a favour to ask you, something I hope you will be able to do for me."

"What is it?" Nicholai asked. "If it's within my power then it shall be done."

"Not now." Joseph smiled, pleased at how readily his friend had made the promise, "Let's get this sorted out," he waved his hand in the direction of the sleigh, "then I'll ask." Intrigued but respectful of Joseph's wishes, Nicholai agreed to these terms and the groundskeeper went off to collect as many lanterns as he could without arousing suspicion and some flints to light them.

"What do you think it is he wants me to do for him?" Nicholai asked the elf as they sat together in the sleigh, waiting for Joseph to get back.

"I have an idea." the elf replied, slyly, "But I'll wait and hear what he has to say."

"Oh?" Nicholai was intrigued.

"I'm not going to say just yet." she smiled at him, "But if I'm right, then he's going to ask you for a gift of sorts for someone else."

"Well," Nicholai beamed, "that's what I'm known for! Speaking of which," he pointed up into the tree, "see what those two have come up with!" The elf looked up and saw the two Pieten sat in a branch above, putting the finishing touches to a crude figurine that they clearly just made.

"That's amazing!" the elf exclaimed. "Not as detailed as the toys we make but look! Its arms and legs move and everything!" Nicholai grinned as he watched her looking up with an expression of awe on her face.

"In my time," he explained to her, "we all work together. You make the pieces of the toys and they put them together like you can see there!"

"But I always thought they were dangerous and destructive!" she exclaimed, feeling a little ashamed of her prejudice. "They've been so helpful to us and, well, I didn't know that they could create like that!"

"They're not destructive at all." Nicholai explained, pleasantly. "They're just very inquisitive. They love finding out how things work. If you think you've seen them breaking things before, they would just have been taking them apart to find out how they work." At the back of his mind, Nicholai was slightly concerned that, by having this conversation, he was affecting the future. However, he had come to accept that things would play out as they always had done since he had, in fact, always been present at this time. He assumed that the elf would be able to keep her new understanding of the Pieten to herself until the time was right for the whole community to embrace them and it didn't feel right to allow her to continue with her misconceptions about his hairy little friends while they were all working together so closely.

Shyly, one of the Pieten scrambled down from the tree and held the doll out to the elf, offering it to her as a gift. He spoke quickly in his own, strange language which Nicholai translated for the benefit of the elf.

"He says they made this for you." he smiled. "He says they felt sad for you being so far away from your friends so wanted to make you a friend to keep you company."

"Tell him I think that's very sweet and I'd be delighted to accept it!" beamed the elf, taking the doll from the Pieten and hugging it tightly, "But please tell him as well that I hope they will be my friends while we are travelling together?" Nicholai relayed this message to the little man who nodded enthusiastically. There was no need for a translation.

"I hope this will be enough!" Joseph called out, emerging through the trees with his arms full of lamps of varying sizes. "It was all I could carry. So," he smiled, seeing the friendly scene between the elf and the two Pieten who were, by now, both sat with her in the sleigh, one on either side, "How do you want to do this?"

Twenty One

Not too long afterwards, Joseph and Nicholai stood either side of Sleipnir, each holding onto the somewhat reluctant beast's reins in one hand and holding a lantern aloft with the other. Behind them, the sleigh slowly trundled along the newly-hewn floor of the tunnel. Nicholai had been a little concerned that dragging it along rocky ground would damage the runners but, as Joseph pointed out, there was enough loose sand carpeting the floor to make the sleigh move almost as smoothly as if it were being pulled through snow. In the sleigh, the elf was sat with a Pieten either side, all three of them clutching lamps to light the tunnel around them.

It amused Nicholai greatly that Sleipnir, who had not seemed in the least bothered by his master's rapid ageing or gaining the ability to fly, should be so spooked by the darkness. It had taken several minutes of coaxing and persuasion before he would even take one step down the ramp into the tunnel and even now, more than half way along the journey, he still seemed very uneasy.

"Not too far to go now." Nicholai assured his equine friend.

Soon enough, they reached the end of the tunnel and found themselves in a dark, high-ceilinged cavern. Holding his lantern higher, Joseph looked from one side to the other before seeing what he was looking for.

"I wasn't quite sure where we came in," he explained, "it took me a moment or two to get my bearings but I see it now. That chamber over there." He dropped the reins and pointed to the far side of the cavern, "That's where we can leave the sleigh. It's quite deep. If we throw the blankets over it then nobody will see it, even if they come poking around down here."

Knowing that it would be hard for the horse to turn around in the chamber which was only a little wider than the sleigh, Nicholai unharnessed Sleipnir and the elf hopped out of the sleigh to stand with him and keep him calm. There would easily be room for Joseph to move around the sleigh while cleaning it up as he had promised but Joseph was quite a bit smaller than Sleipnir. While the elf stood with the horse, Joseph, Nicholai and the two Pieten pushed the sleigh deep into the sandstone chamber. The floor of the cave itself was far less smooth than that of the tunnel so the sleigh did not move as easily but, eventually, the four men managed to get it in place and cover it over with the blankets that Joseph had fetched earlier.

"That should do it!" Joseph smiled, "As I promised, I'll get it cleaned up as best I can, scrape off all the burned parts to give it a chance to repair itself then, when I think I've done all I can., I'll seal it in so that nobody will find it by accident. If all goes according to plan, it will be here waiting for you when you get back to your own time." He beamed proudly and Nicholai held his arms out to give a hug of thanks.

"I don't know how we would have done this without you." Nicholai thanked his oldest friend once more. "But there was something you wanted of me? You said that you would ask once we had hidden the sleigh."

"Ah yes." Joseph smiled but there was sadness in his eyes. "Annalina..." He broke off.

"Yes?" Nicholai asked, a lump forming in his throat as he thought once more of the little girl who would by now have woken up in the cave and started to come to terms with her new life among the elves.

"You said that she is safe? That she is well?"

"I promise you that." Nicholai assured him. "It takes many years, long enough for me to start looking like this," he pointed to his own white-bearded face and chuckled a little, "but I will find her and we will be together again."

"Oh, I believe you!" Joseph waved his hand, "After all I've seen, I have no reason to doubt it. But her parents...." he paused again for a moment, tears in his eyes, as he tried to find the right words. "They've just lost their little girl. They need something to give them hope, to assure them that life is still worth living."

"What would you have me do?" Nicholai asked, "I cannot tell them what has happened or is to happen. They wouldn't understand what has happened to her. She is alive, safe and happy but she isn't a part of their world any more. If I told them where she was then they would want to take her back and it would kill them to learn that they could not."

"I understand that," Joseph explained, "and I'm not asking that you tell them. I'm asking that you show them."

"Show them?" Nicholai exclaimed, "But how can I...?"

"They'll think it was a dream afterwards," explained Joseph, "I'm sure of it. Take them to see her while they are sleeping; wake them up just long enough to see that she is alive and that she is happy. I'm sure you have some way of sending them back to sleep? Or your little friend there does, at any rate?" He grinned at the elf who nodded her confirmation, "When they wake up, back in their own beds, they'll think that they had been dreaming but, when they discuss their dreams as I am sure that they will, they will find that they both had the same dream and will take it as a sign that their little girl is safe. It's not much," he admitted, "but it will give them hope. Will you do it?"

"How could I not?" Nicholai asked, his eyes filled with tears. "I spent so many years of my life believing she was out there somewhere but with nothing more than a feeling in my heart to back that up. If there's anything I can do to make this terrible time a little easier for them, then of course I will do it!"

"You are truly the man I always believed that you would grow up to be." Joseph remarked proudly and the two men hugged again, warmly, in the orange glow of the lantern lights.

"What about afterwards?" Nicholai turned to the elf and asked, "If we're visiting the caves again, would you like me to drop you off there?"

"I told you I would stay with you," she grinned, "until we can find a way to get you back to where you belong! Days here are short at this time of year and it will be getting dark soon. As soon as her parents are asleep we can collect them. I have a powder that will make sure they stay deeply asleep until you choose to wake them up. Once they're safely back in their beds, then we can start looking for that storm."

"Well I don't know about the rest of you," Joseph smiled when he saw that all the formal business was concluded, "but I'm starving and I happen to know a lovely little tavern in the next village where we can get a fine meal, a goodbye celebration if you will, while you wait for the farmer and his wife to fall asleep."

Twenty Two

The grieving father stirred and rubbed his eyes. He was sure that he had fallen asleep in his bed, his wife by his side, but now he seemed to be in the middle of a snow-covered forest, a heavy blanket around his shoulders to keep him from feeling the cold too keenly.

Looking to his side, he saw that his wife was with him, similarly wrapped and also beginning to stir.

"Where are we?" the woman asked her husband.

"I don't know but..." he looked around and saw that they were not alone. A little way off stood a tall man in a long red coat which was trimmed with white fur and decorated with beautiful gold embroidery. His long white hair tumbled around his shoulders and, as he turned to smile at them, they saw that he also had a luxuriously thick, white beard.

Raising his finger to his lips to indicate that they must remain silent, he beckoned them to join him. The confused couple did as they were instructed and stood by the man as he gently pulled back the branches of one of the trees to allow them to see into the clearing beyond. What they saw there almost made them cry out but their mysterious companion held his finger to his lips again, reminding them to stay quiet. In their grief-stricken and confused state, they did as they were told and took in the scene before them.

Flying in circles around the clearing, climbing high then swooping low, weaving in amongst each other were eight deer with magnificent antlers but it was not these spectacular, impossible beasts that held their attention. Instead, the couple were focussed on the small figure sat in the middle of the clearing, looking up at the deer in wonder. It was a young girl with beautiful, long red hair which hung over her shoulder in a plait. She was dressed in a beautiful red dress with white patterns stitched onto it and around her shoulders was a red, fur-lined cloak that spilled out around her as she sat in the snow, enjoying the show that the deer were putting on for her. It was their lost little girl. Their Annalina.

"She's safe now." the white-bearded man assured them, breaking the silence but speaking too softly for the girl to hear. "She'll always be safe here with us. I promise. Remember this scene," he urged them, "and carry it with you always in your hearts. Whenever you feel sad, think of her here and know this," he smiled warmly at them, "I give you my word that you will see her one more time, before your lives are over." With that, he raised his hand, smiled again and blew a fine mist of powder from the palm of his hand into their faces. Both parents wanted to know more, to ask about their little girl, about where they were and what they had seen but already the sleepiness was overwhelming them. The last thing they saw before their eyes closed once more was the smiling, happy face of their beloved daughter, Annalina.

To be continued...

Printed in Great Britain
by Amazon.co.uk, Ltd.,
Marston Gate.